Antonio Ram  of books for adults and lected to participate in tl ival. The project brough nder the age of forty and resulting in the Mexico 2... ...., published by Pushkin Press.

Antonio has received numerous regional and national awards for his writing. On an international level his novel *La guarida de las lechuzas* won the Fundacion Cuatrogatos prize in Miami as well as winning the International Latino Book Award. His YA books have been recommended by IBBY Mexico; *The Wild Ones*, originally published as *Salvajes*, is his third book to be chosen for the White Ravens.

Claire Storey translates from Spanish and German into English. She specialises in literature for younger readers with a particular interest in middle-grade and YA fiction. In 2021/22, she was given funding from Arts Council England for a translation project focusing on Young Adult Literature from Latin America. She regularly volunteers in schools to talk about careers with languages and was named Outreach Champion 2021 by the Institute of Translation and Interpreting.

Claire Storey is also the translator of two other HopeRoad titles: *Never Tell Anyone Your Name* by Federico Ivanier, and *The Darkness of Colours* by Martín Blasco.

THE WILD ONES

Antonio Ramos Revillas

Translated by Claire Storey

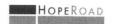

HopeRoad Publishing
17 Kings Avenue
Leeds LS6 1QS

www.hoperoadpublishing.com

First published as **Salvajes**, by Fondo de Cultura Económica Carretera Picacho
Ajusco, 227; 4110 Ciudad de México
First published in Great Britain by HopeRoad in 2024

ISBN: 978-1-913109-34-9
eISBN: 978-1-913109-42-4

*This book has been selected to receive financial assistance from English PEN's PEN
Translates programme, supported by Arts Council England. English PEN exists to
promote literature and our understanding of it, to uphold writers' freedoms around the
world, to campaign against the persecution and imprisonment of writers for stating
their views, and to promote the friendly co-operation of writers and the free exchange
of ideas. www.englishpen.org*

To 'O'

For those who make their lives in the streets
And have survived.
A. R. R.

1

It all started with the road. The road stretching from down there, all the way up here. A straight line. In some places, it's paved, in others it's not. In some places there are concrete walkways, in others there aren't. In the rainy season, black water spills over from the blocked drains at the first opportunity, cutting channels into the road as it rushes down the hill. There are packs of youths and dogs, and a hellish heat that makes you irritable and drowsy.

From the main avenue Eloy Cavazos, Montes Azules Road rises, a broad expanse of twenty metres with litter strewn along the edges. The taxi rank sits at the bottom, with white Beetles from the last century waiting for people who are tired and don't want to walk the twenty-something blocks up the hill. As the road starts to climb, it narrows: twenty metres become fifteen; then down to ten. Scattered along the edges of the road are scrap metal dealers, mechanics' workshops, a meeting place for Alcoholics Anonymous, Roger's frutería, makeshift football pitches, outlets supplying beer to the locals, mountains of debris, gravel on the porches and pavements outside half-built houses, with hardened bags of plaster that create obstacles for the water that pours down the hillside when it rains.

As the road passes Chino's taco stand, a wasteland emerges covered with litter, forgotten tyres and the carcasses of abandoned cars with just the chassis remaining; kids run in and out of them playing cops and robbers, assassins, or soldiers. As you reach the Súper Ocho convenience store about halfway up, the sidewalks become uneven – here a lump of concrete, there just beaten earth. On Thursdays and Saturdays people come here and set out their wares. Dozens of stalls where women, the fayuqueras, sell whatever they can from whatever they've scavenged in exchange for a few pesos: used toys and knick-knacks, or old clothes. Other women shuffle along carrying vegetables taken from the wholesale market or foraged from outside the greengrocer's. And with them come old men selling rusty tools, cables, video cassette tapes, ancient DVD players, Allen keys, screwdrivers, corroded pincers, piles of screws, nails and wrenches in all sorts of shapes and sizes, drill bits for concrete or wood. Some even try to sell those double cassette decks with the dodgy speakers that shake when you turn them up full blast, as old as the hills themselves, as the saying goes.

After that, the road turns to mud and ascends, climbing more narrowly up the hillside, exerting itself, panting, holding its sides, sending more fuel to its lungs to make it all the way up. Almost at the top come the rest of the businesses: tinsmiths, mechanics, cement sellers, video game arcades, barbers who cater to the distinct style of the Kolombias, and Riri's taco stand.

And that's just about where Montes Azules Road ends. It becomes a trickle of stones leading to the hillside's natural terrace we call El Rancho. This is where the market takes place on Saturdays, the overspill from the flea market below. In one corner of El Rancho stands an immense Anacahuita plant, a type of Mexican olive tree, and there's an ancient iron bridge which crosses a gap in the rocks, connecting their colonia with ours.

On the other side of the bridge, the track splits into footpaths where only the people walking along them know the names. The paths are lined with dwellings made from rubbish: shacks with corrugated metal roofs, houses made of wooden planks. The odd few make the most of concrete blocks, while others fashion plastic supermarket bags into windows. The rock's too hard for hammers to crack, so instead of burying the pipes for water and drainage, they just run along the edges of the hillside. There's more garbage, small privies, pens set up among the rocks housing hens or pigs, a few goats, an electronics workshop with an old stripped-down Valiant that's been there since forever.

Until the narrowest path arrives at the very last house in the colonia.

That's where I was when I saw them.

About every three or four weeks, the police would pick up trucks would appear down below. They'd come for someone or other who lived round here, one of the low-level drillers, or maybe one of the farderas, women known for shoplifting, one of those who nicks stuff and hides it in her clothes – down her shirt, up her skirt.

The police'd drive down Eloy Cavazos Avenue with their sirens off, like they do when they want to pass by quietly, under the radar. But it was impossible not to see them coming. They'd always travel in a convoy of five or six patrol cars, one after the other, scared because they know there's a reason why they call those of us who live here *Los Salvajes*, *The Wild Ones*. A whole heap of cops would travel in the cargo beds behind wearing protective helmets and dark glasses, their faces covered from their noses to their chins, armed with riot shields and truncheons that'd double up as walking sticks when they were hiking up the footpaths.

From Eloy Cavazos Avenue, the trucks filed along the beaten asphalt of Montes Azules Road. The effort needed to get up the hill made their gearboxes whirr. It was easy at first – no problem for the engine in third gear – but as they began to go up, the eight cylinders started to complain loudly. The drivers rapidly changed down through the gears 'til they were pressing the gas pedal right down to the floor. The engines spluttered, breaking the silence of the surrounding area. Children appeared out of the nearby houses, chasing the convoy to see what would happen. They'd report back later to their mamás who didn't even break off from washing clothes, watching TV or whatever it was they were doing. They'd seen it all before.

From my viewpoint up above, I watched them too.

The riot police reached the end of the asphalt and parked up in twos and threes by El Rancho. They say the massive Anacahuita was there before the hillside was covered in houses, dogs, workshops and grocery stores, and at this time of day, that plant was the only thing there at all. The cops, the chotas as we call them, climbed out of the pick-ups in groups of six or seven. I watched them jumble together and stagger like goats being herded towards the pens up here. Eventually they sorted themselves out and crossed the bridge towards our colonia. It was too hot; the cloudless sky was pale, so pale, the sunlight immense and bright. I stood up and the breeze wafted my baggy T-shirt, puffed up the legs of my shorts and tickled my toes; I was only wearing flip-flops.

About now, the shadow of the hillside would begin inching down the slopes around us. Our house has always been the first one to get the shade, ever since Mamá and Papá (before they killed him) took ownership of this piece of rock. Ours is also the only one around here with a cement roof. That was a hard Sunday morning's work a few years back, turning stone slabs to reality after Má got hold of some sand, stones and mud bricks donated by one of the local leaders in exchange for votes in the previous elections.

God knows how many times Má must have taken the bus into the city to shout at some council representative or senator, or to stand in the front row at the end of a campaign, long enough for them to stop giving her a sandwich and a glass of orange juice and begin giving her bricks and cement to build the house. That, together with her savings and a loan from someone or other, meant our house was the first in the area to have a proper roof, none of that metal sheeting which makes the summer heat hotter and lets in the rain during the September downpours.

That roof was my mother's pride and joy. We were all proud of it: her, me and my younger brothers, Fredy and Marcos. We were also proud of how hard Má worked. That's not to say the other women didn't work hard – they all did – but she was determined we would study. She didn't want us roaming around or getting involved with the gangs – the Kolombias or the Norteños – or even the graffiti kids, there with an aerosol can in hand ready to spray gates, houses or any wall they could find. For Má, it was all about school, home and homework. She made us study. I was in the third year of high school and went in for the morning session. Fredy was in the first year but had to go in the afternoons because there weren't any other spaces. Marcos also did afternoons, in the fifth year at the school for younger kids.

It wasn't easy though. We couldn't exactly avoid the other kids who lived nearby (and they had it worse than us) so we'd go along with everyone else, we just wouldn't get involved. When we played football, I was good in defence, and my brothers would do odd jobs for some of the guys in the area. We'd struck it lucky really, because they'd killed off most of the old local cartel members, and those who carried on with it all did so on the sly, like my old compa Jeno. He was involved in everything, but in a chilled-out kind of way. The colonias felt calmer too, or so it seemed at least.

Sometimes when I was at school, I'd turn my head and could make out the lower part of the hill. I'd follow it up 'til I could see El Peñón, the big rock where our colonia is. I could just about spot the handful of buildings with their corrugated tin roofs and wooden walls, and further up, beyond where the sun lets you see, I'd find our house: a tiny cube of blue-painted concrete, complete with roof, and on top, fresh laundry, blowing from side to side on the washing line.

I wonder who they're coming for now, I thought to myself. I'd laid out a blanket on the roof to study on, pinning it down with bricks at each corner. I was stuck on a fractions question.

As I was saying, the chotas carried on past El Rancho. In the days when Don Neto ruled the colonia, that's where they'd stop and wait for him. He always had a couple of

7

skinny but agile guys with him, armed with AK-47s and AER15 assault rifles. When things were peaceful between the chotas and the narcos, that let everyone know exactly who was in charge. At El Rancho, they'd swap news, documents and money. Sometimes the chotas would wait, and Don Neto would send his mob for the victim who'd come out fighting, but ultimately go quietly. Nobody wanted to piss the old man off cos they say Don Neto used to help the family afterwards. They'd hand the victim over to the police who'd handcuff them and take them away. But since Don Neto had gone, and with him everyone else, the chotas would barge in like they owned the place, and there was nothing and nobody to stop them. They were so sure of themselves they didn't even take the Marines with them on their patrols any more.

I crossed my arms, watching the police officers' slow ascent, and then went down to eat. Má had made chorizo salsa and the smell was floating up from the kitchen. It's by far the tastiest thing she makes. She fries some chorizo in a pan, grates in tomato, adds lots of onion and slices of chilli, and then she lets it cook down until the mixture's soft and mushy. We pile the salsa and beans onto a hunk of bread. The juice soaks into the soft middle of the bread and tastes amazing.

As I went in, I wondered who they were coming for at this time of day, when the sun and the heat were at their strongest. Jeno? Maybe. Uriel was already in the box, the other lookouts too, so chill. Karen and La More hadn't done anything for ages. My generation were all accounted for, at least. But our old folks had been quiet too. The scuffles with the other colonia didn't count. They weren't serious, almost nothing.

I went in and grabbed a plate.

It wasn't long before I heard the whistles of people warning others to flee before the convoy arrived. I looked out the window and saw several neighbours scarpering (some shirtless, others almost completely naked) in a hurry because the feds were on their way. That's why they never get anyone: while they're on their way up, the people they're looking for are already on their way down, fleeing around the edges of El Rancho.

Má was sweeping the house as usual when the whistles stopped, and she turned to look at me.

'Are they coming for you, Efraín?'

'No, Má. How can you even think that? I've not done anything.'

'Weren't you off with Jeno the other day?'

'Yeah, but we didn't do anything. All we did was go for a drive around Imperial.'

'I don't know why you spend so much time driving around that neighbourhood. You'll find nothing but trouble.'

We went there because that's where one of Jeno's three girlfriends lives. Esther was a year older than us, and she had two really pretty sisters who worked weekends in an ice-cream shop in the city. I'd not had a girlfriend for months (not since Irma dumped me) so I was free. My compa didn't talk to me about his other girlfriends.

Má was holding a small towel which she'd been using to mop the sweat off her arms. It was her day off from cleaning houses, well, other people's. Má barely registered these searches. Neither did we. We were, as she'd always proudly announced, 'honourable people'.

It was just me and her. My little brothers were at school. Perhaps that's why I didn't notice when the cops arrived at our door. There were four of them: worn out from the climb, their helmets crooked, sweating buckets, the buttons almost bursting on their soaking uniforms.

'Hey, kid,' said one. 'This where Miguel Saldívar lives? They told us down there ...'

My heart began pounding in my chest. Miguel was Má's boyfriend. Just then she appeared in the doorway.

'What d'you want him for?'

'We just want to talk to him, señora,' said one officer, the skinniest one.

'He's not here right now. Shall I give him a message?'

The officers in the doorway looked around the house 'til one of them said, 'Hey, Sergeant, that's what we're looking for.'

The mattress. The only new thing we had. I felt the terror, gently at first, then sharp, like a knife at my throat.

They were pointing to the mattress leaning against the wall, the one Miguel had brought to the house a few days before as a present for Má.

'Right then, señora. Step back, please,' came the gruff voice of one of the officers, and as he said this, other officers stepped into the house. One blew his whistle, the echo bouncing off the hillside to reach the ears of the other police officers waiting along the narrow paths.

They were already pushing Má so I sprang towards her, trying to protect her. It all happened so quickly, like a song that suddenly speeds up, so fast it's impossible to sing along because you just can't catch your breath. One officer shoved us up against a wall while another handcuffed Má's wrists behind her back. Some of our belongings fell onto the floor. The fat bodies of the policemen were uncontrollable blue masses, ricocheting around the house. Má began to panic – her face white, her lips like she was dead – but she channelled all her energy into her eyes as she yelled at me, 'Go, run and get your brothers!'

But I couldn't move. I was in shock, paralysed by the anger and fear of seeing Má like that.

'Look, Sergeant, there's the label. The numbers match, it's the one.'

Má tried to wriggle free, but the guard held her tight. Me? I was motionless, just one more rock on the hillside.

'Take it away,' ordered the sergeant.

That mattress! The effort it had taken to get it all the way up from the main road, carried on our backs pretty much the whole way.

Má had asked Miguel for it. She'd told him, 'I could buy it, but I want to know if you're willing to contribute anything to this home.' Miguel knew we needed mattresses because there weren't enough for us all. We only had one that he and Má used. When Miguel went home, back down the hill to his mamá, my youngest brother slept on it too. Fredy and I slept on two strips of foam which didn't do much to soften the hardness of the concrete floor. The floor was another of Má's great joys because the rest of the houses nearby just had well-trodden gravel or sand floors.

'What are you doing? Listen, wait!' Má yelled as they led her out of the house, handcuffed. 'What's going on? Hey, no!'

The police carried on as they do. As we all know they do. They didn't stop, even though Má was begging them. They didn't rest 'til they'd removed the mattress from the house and leaned it up against an outside wall.

'Stop yelling, señora. That mattress is here, and guess what, it's in your house. And anyway, who said you could live here? This hillside is government property. Where are your papers? Your documents?'

Má was overcome with fear. I saw her suddenly droop. Nobody in our area had papers for anything, we were all winging it. If you got there first and found somewhere to live, you held onto it and built your house with whatever you could find. They could throw us all out without even lifting a finger. I turned to look at the house. All Má's hard work had been turned to nothing. Everything was broken, our clothes were strewn across the floor, the table destroyed. The bread had been trodden on and the chorizo salsa was splattered up the wall. Some of the officers heaved the mattress onto their shoulders.

'We'll have to take you in, señora,' the sergeant said eventually and gave the order to move her. I took a couple of steps as if to follow; my legs were shaking and I was drenched in a cold sweat, my pulse slack. The music in my head was now playing in slow-mo, like one of those sloweddown songs the Kolombianos listen to. Má's mournful voice asking them to stop was getting weaker and weaker. And all I could say was, 'Leonor! Leonor! Mamá!'

I just watched as they began to lead her along the footpath, past the mistrustful eyes of the neighbours, who had come out to witness the fray.

The house finally fell silent as Má continued to move further away. I finally managed to drag myself out of the trance, but there were still a couple of chotas hanging around. One grabbed me by the arm and threw me against the wall. I got up again and the other one punched me in the cheek. It felt like a block of steel and bone slamming into my face. I landed on the floor, my head spinning from the blow. I couldn't speak or see because of the fire burning in my head. I tried to stand up, but the room seemed to have moved somewhere else. I put my hand out to try and find something to defend myself with, but I was still on the floor and all I could find was a torn green blanket. Má had spread it over the mattress so it didn't get dirty. That's why she'd leaned it up against the wall too, so we didn't tread on it.

Má didn't like us fighting but I'd seen enough with the gangs to know that throwing a stone at someone gave you enough time to escape, help a friend or put someone in their place. Shouting caused confusion but did absolutely nothing at all to help. So I turned and grabbed something off the floor: a cup. But just as I was about to throw it, I was hit in the face with the butt of a rifle. Blood flowed, blocking my nostrils. I began to cough. I inhaled as deeply as I could through my mouth, but my tongue was on fire. I spat a couple of times, then the smell of chlorine hit the back of my throat. Someone picked me up just to throw me on the floor again. I fell flat on my face and felt a boot on the back of my neck.

'Let's go,' said the other cop.

Through the open door, I could see as the mattress and Má began their descent, escorted by the police. The same scene was repeated time after time, day after day, month after month. Má was a drop in the ocean. That image would stay with me. I watched them disappear, fading from view, vanishing into the hillside, as if Má and the officers were ghosts.

'Don't move, perro,' said the guy with his foot on me. 'Stay right there.'

But I didn't. As soon as the last cop had left the house, I took off after them.

2

You're eight years old and you know: you have to look out for the chotas.

You're nine and you know: the chotas'll come at night and get into your house. If you're not careful, they'll screw you over.

You're ten and you're learning: throw stones at the chotas – at them, at their cars – as they pass by. Then run as fast as you can, so they won't catch you.

You're eleven and you've learned: anyone can run faster than some, fat, old, bored policeman whose only weapon is a truncheon to hit you with because they can't use their gun to kill you.

You're twelve and you realise: they control the business too. They decide who works and who doesn't. You watch them drink in some bar with a neighbour of yours. There's an agreement. You know it. Everyone knows it.

You're thirteen and you make a mistake: they come for you. It's worse for others; they put them in the slammer.

You're fourteen and you're out of the slammer, but they've got you on their radar: they've seen you. They know who you are. You're theirs. They're going to take you in whenever they can: you're carrying something in your bag and you look suspicious; you're waiting for a bus; you're shopping down on the avenue; you're here and Los Salvajes can only mean trouble.

You're fifteen and you've heard stories from the others, about how the law doesn't apply to you. You know these stories are true, but you survive.

Until the day they throw your mamá in jail.

3

Pins and needles crept up my right arm. The police didn't hang around; it was too hot. The fierce sun was beating down on the city. I weighed up my options. I hunted for my trainers and stuffed my feet into them as quickly as I could. I left by the back door so they wouldn't see me.

I don't know why I started thinking about Má, picturing her cleaning a huge steel stove in the kitchen of one of the houses where she worked. Next image: her cleaning a living room. Then I imagined her outside our house, fanning herself as she sat on that big, old rock by the door, her tired feet in a bucket of cold water. It hurt so much because in my head, she was already dead. When they took her, it was like the cops had killed her.

That idea fired me up. The hatred I carried inside me was now fed by Má's voice as she begged them to let her go. When Jeno gets angry, his rage is directed at everyone and everything. That's how I felt now. Or perhaps it was more like Don Neto's fury when – so they say – he'd hand someone over who didn't want to go. Or maybe it was the pure, clean anger that everyone in the colonia showed when they took away people you didn't want them to take.

I set off running along the edge of the colonia and saw them arrive at the metal bridge linking El Peñón with the rest of the houses. Them, Má and the mattress. I took the narrow path down one side of El Rancho. A few bushes stood guard in front of piles of rotting food where three loose pigs were enjoying a feast. Close by stood three cows grazing on the plateau, near the rocky edge. As I reached the first house in the colonia below, I left the path, darting along a narrow alleyway that led to another street. I finally popped out on Montes Azules Road just as the vehicles were heading back down in their convoy. Má was in the last one, the mattress in the cargo bed behind. I turned to look back up the hillside and spotted my house with its concrete roof.

I tried to catch up with them, my footsteps pounding in time with my heartbeat. A couple of dogs came out from one of the houses and chased me but, being more agile, I left them behind. The steep gradient of Montes Azules pushed me along as I rushed down the hill. I almost caught up with the pick-ups. One of the cops looked at me indifferently, a machine gun resting in his lap.

When Má saw me, a smile flickered across her face, but then she made a gesture, ordering me to go back. *If Don*

Neto were here, none of this would have happened, I thought. He never let them take the colonia's women. Youths, yes, he'd hand them over without a second thought. He had a bit more consideration for the men, but he never gave them the señoras or the farderas, the women shoplifters.

I ignored Má's plea and carried on chasing the vehicle until one of the chotas – the one riding standing up with one foot on the bumper and one foot in the cargo bed – pointed his machine gun at me, gesturing with his other hand for me to stop. Má tried to get to her feet but couldn't. I stopped, fired up by rage and ashamed of my slow reaction, but with my gaze fixed firmly on the barrel of the gun that was trained on me just a few metres away. I decided to focus on information instead and made a mental note of the patrol number: 4538-A.

They moved one street further along and I began to run again. I followed the convoy as quickly as I could along the uneven walkways, far from the gaze of the chotas. The vehicles moved slowly because going down the hillside with your foot on the gas was just asking for trouble. When they got to Eloy Cavazos Avenue, they turned on their blue lights to stop the traffic then crossed over into the central lane and swept off in a line down to the city.

I wanted to rip my head off and toss it in the gutter. I wished I was down there, drowning in desperation. I wanted those same dogs that had chased me to come now and pick my head up with their teeth and chew it until they were done. I wanted … I wanted … I wanted … I wanted … I wanted to scream, but the shame of it all blocked my voice. My legs gave way. It felt like I'd been winded, a huge pain in the belly, the sort that makes you puke. Pure fear. Pure savage fear that turns your insides to water.

Then I remembered Miguel, his mattress and how we'd got it up the hillside. How clever we thought we were. 'I could buy it myself,' Má had insisted. 'but what I want to know, Miguel, is if you're willing to contribute anything to this home.'

The convoy pulled away into the distance. I looked around. I had no money for the 209 bus, less still for a taxi. Only then did I notice my sweat-soaked T-shirt and the pain from having been beaten up back at the house. The chase had deadened the sting, but now it was starting to creep into my bones and my nerves, like burns beneath the skin. I touched my nose. It felt bloody, maybe it was even broken. The pain wrapped itself around my ankles and paralysed my waist. My hands were covered in a mixture of dust and still-warm blood. My face burned and I struggled to breathe. Then, in the middle of this tense desperation, I heard a whistle. Jeno had just appeared behind me.

'They took your old woman, your jefa,' he said casually. 'Nobody stood up for her, fucking cowards!'

'D'you know where they've taken her?' I asked him.

'Yeah. C'mon, I'll take you.'

4

For the first part of the bus journey, I could feel my hands sweating from the anxiety, and my feet tapped nervously against the metal floor. An electric current had taken root in my elbows. A flicker of electricity, like when you burn your fingers changing the fuses and your hands light up. As the 209 made its way, Jeno's laid-back attitude started to rub off on me, helping me to take back control of my body.

But nothing eased my internal anxiety, much less the people jammed in together down the bus aisle. There weren't any seats free and every time the bus sped up or slowed down, we pressed into the other standing passengers around us. The tightly-packed bodies and arms created an animal with many heads and limbs, one single animal squeezed in between the seats. So many heads. So many hands. So many faces all turned to look in different directions. Gazes fixed on the street, or the neckline of a girl sitting down, or the bus windows, or the roof, or the letters saying 'Exit' stuck to the back door, or a TV magazine. Concentrated looks, lost in the nothingness of ensuring you didn't make eye contact with anyone else in the cramped space on the bus.

The seconds I was stuck on the 209 mirrored the long, terrified seconds Má spent in the chotas' patrol pick-up. They must have been miles away by now, but Jeno still tried to reassure me. 'They won't do nothing to her, just give her a scare. They don't mess with the señoras.'

That's what I was thinking about when the bus stopped. God knows why it stopped, but it did. Jeno leaned over to the window, opened it, stuck out his head – much to the annoyance of the guy next to it – and reported there'd been an accident up ahead.

'Let's get off,' I said to him.

''K,' he replied, without asking why.

I was eating myself up inside. My guts were churning to the point of giving me backache. The pain was twisting and shooting upwards, trying to make a hole in my belly, like in Mortal Kombat when they rip out the loser's spine through his mouth.

'Pinche Efraín, chill out!' Jeno swore once we were back on the street, but that was his only complaint. 'If I know anything, they'll let your old má go. Makes no difference if you rush – rushing don't exist where they're taking her. Hold up!'

The bus was on a bridge crossing the Silla river and the queue of cars at a standstill snaked along both sides. The air was filled with the sound of dozens of horns being honked up and down the road. The sound came and went. It would start at the back of the queue and then ripple forwards to the site of the accident at Kentucky Road. As we walked, out of the corner of my eye I watched the bus passengers. Crammed in. Motionless. They'd be waiting God knows how long, and all because they didn't want to pay another ten pesos to get a different bus. Or perhaps they were too lazy to walk in the sun. Jeno took out some chewing gum from his pocket and shared it with me. The blueberry flavour mingled with my saliva.

'We're never going to get there,' I swore as we walked.

'You worrying isn't gonna get your jefa out,' Jeno replied with all the experience of someone who'd been locked up several times. 'But if they lock her up, soon as you talk to her, tell her not to give up. If she keeps her head down, she'll be fine.'

We reached the other side of the bridge. Beneath us ran shallow, fast-flowing water with grass growing along the banks. A few weeks before, a downpour had nearly washed away the city. The water had gushed along the roads and paths, restless and muddy. Living on the hillside had certain benefits, like the view, or being the first in the city to get any shade, but during the rains, nature took its revenge. The water fell with such fury, the best thing to do was to create channels for it to flow down, and then just wait. We'd watched terrified as a cascade spilt out right next to our house. Like a rockfall that starts with a pebble and picks up more and more stones on the way down, the flow of water grew and grew, the water expanding. It needed more space! Eventually the water broke through the rocks and poured into a stream headed towards the path and away from our house – luckily for us. Such were the problems of living up on a hillside. The other problems were wildlife. Loads of it everywhere: mosquitos, cockroaches, rats. Once, even a fox got into the house and rubbed its mangey self all over some blankets Má had just laid out.

A few metres ahead we saw the accident. Three cars. Two had crashed into each other and the third had gone into a lamp post. They spread across two of the three lanes while the other road users now squeezed through the single free lane. Jeno wandered towards the owners. They were all on their phones, probably speaking to their insurance companies. It was a funny scene: the owners, pissed off, with their phones stuck to their ears like a huge tragedy had occurred, and Jeno, off to one side, taking a good look at the dents in the cars.

Suddenly, he made a beeline for one of the car doors and stuck his hand through the open window of the Seat Ibiza. One of the men spotted him and yelled. Jeno leaped back and started running. I went after him, crossing the road and dodging cars. Jeno – expert in escaping – bounded quickly away. He always ran like that, like he was bouncing, ready for one big leap to take him far away from his pursuers.

I didn't catch up with him 'til he slowed down and threw himself onto a bench under the shade of a tree a few streets away. When I reached him, he was breathing heavily, but a few minutes later he let out a whoop of laughter.

'Did you see them? Did you see the old bastard?'

While he was laughing, he showed me the wallet and car keys, one of those electric ones. That car wasn't going anywhere, and the traffic would only get worse. We pulled out the ID card. The Seat's owner was called Gonzalo Fernández Garza. He lived in a colonia not far from here, one of the gated residential areas with security guards at the entrance: Laurel de la Montaña. In the photo on his ID, he looked angry. He also had money, store cards for Costco and Sam's department store, two credit cards, a debit card and a photo of a woman and child.

'That's gotta be his wife and kid ... but let's see,' Jeno announced, rummaging around in a tiny pocket where he found a picture of another woman, much younger than his wife. She had a clear complexion, long hair, pretty cheekbones, couldn't have been older than twenty-five. 'She must be his girlfriend.'

She was pretty. Her lips were painted red. On the back of the photo was a name: Cora. We threw away the cards, Jeno said we didn't have time to go and blow it all at the supermarket. We also left behind the driver's licence but held onto the photos and the money. Six hundred and seventy pesos would help us to get where we needed more quickly.

We took a short cut through the colonia and came out on a different avenue, but not before Jeno had stopped to buy a cola for himself, and nick another for me. We tried to get a taxi, but nobody would stop. I don't exactly blame them. Jeno and I were both dark and skinny. Jeno was wearing baggy trousers, a gold chain hung around his neck and his hair was shaved on the back with long, bleached – almost scorched – locks at each temple. As for me, I may have been wearing very normal clothes, shorts and an oversized T-shirt, but I definitely didn't look like I had any money. And then there was the matter of the injury to my face, though the swelling had started to go down a bit.

In the end, an old guy gave us a lift on the condition we paid in advance. We told him where we were going and he smiled sarcastically, as if that's where people like us *would* be going. The taxi zipped along. The warm air breezed in through the window because the driver didn't want to turn on the air con. Jeno kept looking at the photos of the two women and the girl.

'The wife's prettier,' he said.

'I like the other one,' I said, grabbing at the photo but missing it, just as a gust of air caught it and swept Cora away for ever.

'Seriously?!' he complained, swearing at me.

I'd never liked those photos, the kind you need for certificates or ID cards. They reveal something strange, a certain look, like freezing people in time. People who are scared – like rabbits caught in headlights – but who are desperately trying to make themselves look good. People who end up caught out by a camera which only shows the truth, that we're all just useless creatures. The only photos I kept of Papá were the ones from his ID cards, and they don't show him at his best. I don't even remember his funeral. The wake was at a house in a colonia on the other side of the city, a house they lent to Má because she didn't have money for anything else. He used to work as a watchman on a construction site and some of his workmates came along. My grandma and an uncle came too, but nobody else. At the end, one of the engineers turned up with an envelope for Má with some money in it from a whip-round they'd done, but that was it.

'What's the wife called?' Jeno asked me.

'Dunno.'

'Well, I'll scan them later and see if they come up on Google. Y'know you can find out anything on there. One of my compas managed to work five thousand pesos out of some old grandma the other day, just by using the stuff he found on Facebook. Stupid idiots! But great for us that such idiots even exist.'

'Maybe,' I said to myself, but thinking about it hurt. Maybe that was Má's problem. Perhaps she was stupid for ever having trusted Miguel. Love's a bitch. And don't I know it.

5

For weeks, Má had been complaining to Miguel about how fed up she was that Fredy and me had to sleep on the floor. It wasn't like her to keep going on about something like that, like she was expecting someone else to deal with it, but that day, the whole bed thing was getting her down and she was cross and miserable. It hadn't been a problem before – my brothers had slept on a mattress with Má while I'd slept on a foam mat. But when Má started seeing Miguel, well, they kicked the boys out. That's how it'd been for several months – them on the mattress and us sharing the mats, plumping them up with blankets – until one night when Má and Miguel had a bust-up outside. He was trying to get her to calm down, but she had a plan, so she chased him off. 'Go and sleep with your brothers,' she started, before going in for the kill. 'I could buy a mattress myself, but I want to know if you're willing to contribute anything to this home, invest something in it. I'm not interested in knocking about with some old, kept man.'

Miguel didn't leave straight away; he stood out there for a while, smoking in the darkness. The smell of burning tobacco wafted in through the window but was soon dispersed by the gusts of wind coming down the hillside. At that time of night, you could hear the crickets.

On the hillside, silence doesn't exist. There's always something vibrating, whether it's an insect, a rattlesnake or even the air itself. I don't know if the air on the hills has a name, but it should, a pretty one, like *cascade*, a word that sounds like it's vibrating. Hundreds and thousands of tiny gusts, merging together, like water when a crack opens in the rock, a trickle growing bigger and bigger. That's how the air is on the hillside. You know it's brand new, sucked up from the depths of the earth, the scent of rocks and roots, an air – sometimes cool – that passes you by, then picks up pace, moving everything, calling out, saying, 'I am the air, listen to me', and, as it flows, it stirs the branches of the trees, the clothes on the washing lines, the flags of the neighbours' favourite teams fluttering above their houses, or the bin bags.

A bird twittered in the night. It must have been about one in the morning when I finally heard Miguel stand up and head down the hillside. Má hadn't closed her eyes the whole time he was there. Only once he'd left did I hear her snoring peacefully.

The best thing about living where we live is the view. Sometimes I drag my mat out and sleep on the roof.

From up there I can watch the city at night, the lights, some motionless, some moving along the avenues like blood flowing through the veins of some ancient animal. Sometimes, I think that's what we are, lights travelling briefly along a broad avenue before getting lost in the night. Towards the south of the city, you can make out a fire up high in the air, the chimneys of the Cadereyta refinery that never go out. I can see the aeroplanes too, as they arrive at the airport on the outskirts of the city. The red dots blink on the horizon before they crash into the ground. One day I'll buy myself some binoculars so I can watch them land. We've never been to the airport – we don't even know how to get there – but it can't be that difficult. There'll be some bus route that'll take us there. It'd be sick to work in a place like that, watching the planes coming and going, people arriving, people leaving. And hearing the planes too! When I think about them, it seems like magic, I mean, they're so heavy, so how do they get up into the air and stay there?

Round here, when you finish high school, the usual thing is to go and get a full-time job doing whatever you can to make some money. Nearly all my compas have a part-time job somewhere – some help out on the taco stands or as a mechanic's apprentice, others deliver parcels for Walmart while some sell newspapers. That's what you do when you decide to take the hard path. If you take the easy path, you make money quickly with no effort at all, but you end up selling yourself along with it.

I've done some odd jobs, helping out quite a few of the men in the colonia. Sometimes, when I'm in a thinking mood, I'll sit and watch the city, watch my colonia, the house where I live, the pigs that graze near the ravine (I always hope one of them will fall over the edge so the owner will cook it, make it into carnitas and share it with us). I'm fifteen and I already know I don't want to live like this for ever, hand to mouth, feeling hungry and sleeping on the floor. I like the hillside, but I want to live down there where the streets are straighter, where the drains don't get blocked, where a different kind of quietness breathes.

That's why when Miguel told us he'd bought a mattress, my brothers and I got all excited. We headed down to the avenue to wait for him by the white taxi rank. We were there nearly an hour before Miguel turned up in Rico's old Ford pick-up. From the window he ordered, 'Climb in, Martínez,' – he always spoke to us using our dad's surname. 'Rico'll take us as far as he can.'

We clambered up happily. Rico was grinning. He's the guy with a pick-up who helps just about everyone to transport their heavy stuff, like fridges, or beds – he's one of the good guys. The mattress was amazing, thick, soft and white, with some sort of topper sewn on, all shrink-wrapped from the factory. We were standing up in the back because the rear part of the Ford had a metal box in it so the mattress barely fit. The breeze ruffled our hair and Fredy and Marcos could barely contain their excitement, but the pick-up only got halfway up the hillside, and there it stopped.

'Never mind, Martínez,' said Miguel, resigned. 'We got this far at least. We'll walk the rest.'

Rico apologised too, but that's just how it is with transporting furniture.

Miguel was tall and slender, and his skin was ruddy from working in the sun. His jobs never lasted long and during slow times, he'd often go to stand with the other men outside the San Pedro market and offer his services by the day. For three hundred pesos he could unload a lorry, rip out a bathroom, clear away debris, whitewash a wall or mow an overgrown field, whatever was needed. He was a tiler too, and like other neighbours, he'd rent the cutting tools because buying new was expensive. After working, he'd spend the money on beer and food, although every so often he'd pitch in something at home. Who knows what Má saw in him because sometimes she nagged him even more than she nagged us. They'd been together for about two years, more or less. Sometimes he'd go off to other cities to look for work, or he'd help out a lorry-driving cousin of his who only paid in dinners. When you've got nothing else, even that's earning.

We jumped out the back of Rico's Ford and between the four of us, we took out the mattress. It was heavy but it didn't matter. It was ours.

'Careful, Martínez. Watch how you're dragging it, Martínez! Come on, heave!'

Let's just say Fredy and Marcos aren't exactly strong. Neither am I. So Miguel decided to shift the mattress from vertical to horizontal, him pulling and lifting from the front with part of it heaved up onto his shoulder, Fredy and Marcos on each side and me on the end pushing. We kept going up, but every ten or twelve metres we had to stop. Then we'd try it again, but the weight of it, together with our sweaty hands and the plastic covering, meant the mattress wobbled all over the place and threatened to land on the floor, almost always on my end. Miguel had never raised his voice to us – he knew it was a right he didn't have – but that afternoon, he looked ready to give us a roasting on more than one occasion.

'Chingado, Martínez!' He swore. 'Has studying made you all soft or something?' Miguel got so frustrated with us that halfway up, he yelled at us to stop. 'Wait here,' he ordered before he disappeared into the streets of the colonia. When he came back, he had three men we didn't know with him, about the same age as Miguel and definitely stronger than us.

'My brothers,' he said eventually. They did look similar, that same thin nose, the forehead, early grey hairs. They were like Miguel, just older or younger versions.

'Leonor's kids?' one of them asked.

'The Martínez brothers, yeah, weedy little things. They're gonna mess this whole damn thing up if they keep knocking it about like this,' responded Miguel, who was in his forties like Má, but could easily be mistaken for fifty, his whole life.

We didn't know much about his family, only that he was the middle child. His jefa – his boss, as we call our mamás – lived down below, but we didn't know her.

With the extra help, we set back to it. We got as far as El Rancho where we stopped for a while in the shade of the Anacahuita.

'Nearly there,' said Miguel and turned to look back down the hill towards the avenue. 'We've done the worst bit.'

But the worst was yet to come. Up to that point we'd been walking on a proper road, on concrete, but from here on up, we'd have to watch our footing on the stones, the uneven ground, the waste water gushing down the hillside in hurried channels. I glanced at Miguel's brothers. They looked tired too.

'How about a beer to gather our strength?' one of them asked.

'Yeah, Mike, send the kids to get us some drinks. We're gasping!'

'Hey, Martínez,' Miguel said, and the three of us jumped to attention.

Miguel's brother took out a fifty and told Fredy to get the drinks. My brother didn't know what to do, so I plucked the note from his hand and sent Fredy to ask for two empty caguamas, the almost one-litre bottles the beer came in. Off he went and came back a few minutes later with two used caguamas. I picked them up, took them to Isra's store and exchanged the empties for ice-cold beers, drops of water still dripping down the sides as I handed them over to the brothers. One of the men ran a bottle across his forehead, the other held it to his chest. I've always been impressed by people who can open a bottle with pretty much anything: forks, the blade of a knife, a stone, a piece of cardboard. Miguel's brothers peeled off the stickers using their nails, then used them as a lever to open the bottles. They sighed an *Aaaah* of relief as they took long, refreshing pulls on the bottles.

Maybe we'd have stayed there, but just then Má appeared at El Rancho. She usually leaves for work really early – like five a.m. early – so she can get over to Contry, or further, to Brisas by six thirty. She stays there until three thirty at the latest, then goes to sell shoes at some offices.

A lot of people know Má because she's like Francisca – the woman from one of our Spanish books – who Death comes for, but never manages to catch up with because Francisca is constantly going from one place to another for work. It has its plus points because it means Má sometimes comes home with clothes, or strange things to eat that she's been given in the houses she cleans. She never asks for them, she told me once, but when people have so much, they get rid of stuff without asking themselves if someone else might need it. In fact, the fridge we used to have, even though it was tiny, had been a gift from a guy who Má worked for, cleaning his office. His work wasn't going well so he closed the office. He didn't want to take all the stuff with him, so he gave the fridge to Má.

Má was knocked for six when she saw us at El Rancho sitting on a mattress while Miguel and his brothers sat off to one side making good work of the caguamas. She came over very deliberately and smiled when she saw what we were bringing up.

'Leonor,' said Miguel, who had leaped to his feet as soon as he saw her. 'A promise is a promise. Um, these are my brothers.'

I could tell Má was excited to meet Miguel's family. They ran through their names, said hello, and then she ordered us to keep going.

'Right then, Martínez, you heard your mother. Back to work.'

We set out on the path again, crossing the metal bridge. Fredy went to drop off the empty bottles and caught up with us further on. Several times we had to find a different route because of all the cables dangling in our path that some of our neighbours used to tap into the main electricity supply.

We were absolutely exhausted when we got there. Má had swept the space where the mattress was to go, next to the other one, but not right up close. She'd unrolled some flowery sheets and once we finally placed it on the floor, she quickly made the bed. Fredy went to throw himself on top, but Má stopped him.

'Just because it's covered in plastic, don't you go thinking you can climb on it all dirty like that. You can have a wash later on and then get in.'

'Hey, old lady,' Miguel called to her. 'I promised my brothers a cook-up if they helped me get it up here. Have you got a couple of pesos for a few sausages?'

Má pretended to be annoyed, a reproach that couldn't hide how happy she was inside. She handed over a one-hundred-peso note, and Miguel told Marcos to go with him to Isra's store to buy some meat and more beers.

While they were gone, Miguel's brothers gathered some sticks and dry leaves to make the fire. They set it not too far from the house, near a path with a view of some caves higher up the hillside. Back when the narcos from the cartels were around, Don Neto's boys used to hide their stuff there, or even themselves after a shoot-out. We called it the times of fire – la lumbre – because back then the whole city was under fire with killings, persecutions and violence; they only ever resolved matters with bullets.

The brothers and Miguel spent the whole afternoon and into the evening eating and drinking nearby. Miguel came in for the little table and took it outside and for a while they sat playing cards. Their laughter floated inside, along with the aroma of the cooking meat. Marcos and Fredy had already washed and they left the water in the tub for me. I dunked myself in it to freshen up. At about ten o'clock, Miguel's brothers poked their heads in to say goodbye, but Má was already asleep. The air outside felt fresh. The crickets' song filled the hillside, as if they were reclaiming their territory in the night, and the sound they produced began to lull me to sleep, like rainwater pattering on the warm sheet metal.

Miguel, tired and tipsy, went to climb into bed next to Má, but as she was already fast asleep, she didn't even notice. We heard him fart a few times before his guts finally gave it a rest. We'd managed something for dinner, a few scraps of leftover meat and sausage, washed down with cola. The mattress was so soft, and I slept so well that night, like I'd finally reached the fluffy, white clouds that sometimes gather over the top of the hill, cool clouds that would disappear with the first light of day.

6

As I went over the events of that day, I felt like such a fool. The taxi dropped us off outside the ministerio público, the first stop for people who've just been arrested. Jeno crossed himself like he was in a church because, he said, it was the first time he was walking in through these doors on his own account and not handcuffed for some 'misunderstanding'.

The five-storey building had a harsh concrete façade with small windows on the top half of each level. You could only see through the first window: a thick internal wall with a door guarded by a police officer seated at a small table, and a metal detector. Lots of people were waiting by the main entrance, lawyers came and went, while other people stopped off to buy cigarettes, chewing gum, sunflower seeds and mints from the sellers who had laid out their wares on the ground in the gardens. The access door for the patrols was on one side of the building, protected by female officers, a grey ramp leading to the upper floors.

'S'where they take you,' Jeno informed me seriously. 'Your jefa must be in there. Let's have a sniff around and see if we can find the Boss.'

The Boss was the lawyer who'd helped Jeno in the past, either getting him off the hook completely, or making sure he spent no more than thirty-six hours locked up. Once he'd even managed to get Jeno out of the correctional. They'd met thanks to a human rights assistant and since then, Jeno had always gone to him for help.

Jeno wasn't stupid. I'd known him since he was a small-time thief and I'd watched him rise up the ranks in the colonia. He started off as a lookout before Don Neto set him up in a trap house selling weed with some other kids from the colonia. He'd invited me to join them, but I said no because Má would've killed me and besides, I was only like eleven and nobody ever took us seriously. Jeno went from being an errand boy to passing drugs by taxi from one part of the city to another. The first time I saw him with a gun I was too scared to ask him if he'd used it, although he must've read my mind because he told me it was 'just in case'.

Where we live, it's not hard to get your hands on a weapon. They don't just give them out like sweets, mind you, but you know who can get you one in exchange for your loyalty. Just like having a girl turned you from a little kid into a respected bro, having a gun was simply another rite of passage. At one point, loads of people had them and kept taking them to school and showing them off during break. Jeno didn't show off because Don Neto told him not to – the ones who survive are the ones who keep quiet, he said.

But then the war began. Right from the first few scuffles, I knew it wouldn't be long until Jeno either disappeared or got killed, but when the war began, la lumbre began to heat up, and everyone started to disappear. Jeno hid, or rather, he slowed his rhythm right down and left the colonia for a year or so. Sometimes I wondered if he'd become a hitter, but something told me he hadn't. During those months in a different neighbourhood, living at his aunt's house, he told me he'd started studying properly, doing this and that. He'd even started running with his uncle, 5k a day. He lived half his life keeping a low profile and the other half with his ear glued to the ground just waiting for a good time to return.

When he came back, Don Neto had gone, and things had started to calm down. Jeno went back to what he'd been doing before, but in a more inoffensive way. He started high school, passed the first year, but then they put him away in the correctional. He came back for the second year and was going to pass the third, although having missed a year, by then he was already the age I am now. Whenever the chotas took him in it was for trivial things.

Sometimes the patrols picked him up for no other reason than they wanted to take some money off him and beat him up because if there's one thing you can count on, it's that the cops will *always* find a reason. Could be your hair – however you decide to wear it – could be your trousers, could be you're standing with your compas on the corner having a laugh. Could be you've just finished work and you look like you've got money in your pocket. They get annoyed if you're on your own, standing waiting for the bus, and the only way they can soothe their irritation is by giving you a good beating when they stop you, when they pick you up, when they're taking you somewhere or when they're letting you go. Well-aimed blows, straight to your torso. Jeno showed me the bruises once, orange-coloured and firm on his dark skin. If there was one thing that united us, it was the colour of our skin, the copper-coloured race as they say on the radio, more the colour of the earth than the pulp of an apple. This colour that turns even more coppery once it's been toasted in the heat of the sun all day. Doesn't matter how we dress, like the scars on a warrior's face, our skin gives us away. And then there were the other clues: our hair almost completely shaved, except for a free-hanging lock on the right; big, oversized T-shirts; baggy trousers, usually hanging below your belly button to reveal the elastic of your boxers, with red Converse on your feet, the ones with the stars, a dazzling bottom half.

It was noisy inside the ministerio público. There were printers, telephones, an advert for the government's Integral Family Development programme playing on a TV screen, before being replaced with others about the legal procedure with lawyers speaking into the camera. I followed Jeno as I tried to get my head around all the different offices and departments. We reached a booth and he asked where to find the lawyers who help people like us, the ones who can't afford to pay. The man, his face tough and red with small ears and thick lips, made a tasteless joke and shook his head. Jeno gave the lawyer's name, but the employee insisted he hadn't seen him.

'We're looking for a lady who's been brought in from El Peñón,' I interrupted.

'Could be anyone. You could try user services over in Criminal,' the man grudgingly replied. 'They bring so many of them here that sometimes they don't all fit, so they take them straight down to the prison instead.'

'Lemme try and get hold of the Boss,' insisted Jeno. 'Just need to see if someone'll lend me a charger. I used to know his number but then he changed it and my phone's dead.' With that, Jeno disappeared.

I recognised myself in the faces of the first-timers, the people who really cared about their family members who had been arrested, desperation tattooed on their faces, anxiety forming a clumsy line across their foreheads. Urgency, anger, fear all visible in their eyes. Others, by contrast, were simply calm, or irritated.

If one of the cops ever asked me where I was off to, I froze, but others didn't. Like when they caught Karen for the millionth time. She knew they'd let her go again in exchange for the same old thing. Or knowing that as a girl, she'd only be inside for a couple of days before they let her go because they needed the space inside for the sicarios, the hitmen they really couldn't release. There was only one time I remember seeing the girls looking really worried, after a mass shooting that killed twenty. There'd been inside help – a couple of the chotas had let some guys into the cells with their guns. The girls were all in a panic. They didn't want to go back inside, but they just couldn't stop themselves going to the shops and stuffing clothes up their shirts or checking other people's pockets for wallets.

I returned to the entrance of the building and asked for the criminal lawyers' office. They gave me a numbered ticket and directed me to a waiting room where there were even more people. Fat people, thin people, women with tired faces, dirty crumpled clothing, old trousers, scruffy shirts, cowboy boots, battered Converse. That's all we were, worn-out clothes sitting on seats. Inside us was the filth of fear.

Jeno reappeared a while later and even as he walked in, I noticed the other people in the waiting room shift uneasily. There's no mistaking Jeno – just glancing at him, you know he'll try to rob you, you don't even need to look hard. There's something in the way he walks, talks and looks that gives him away.

'Managed to charge it. Lemme call him.'

Jeno squeezed in next to me and I watched him stab the numbers into his phone.

'Boss? Hey, how are you, Bossman? Nah, nah, what d'you mean? Yep, no … Yeah, I'm down at the rat trap, but nah, a compa's jefa … Think so … yeah … a-ha … yeah … The chotas came and took her … Um, dunno … with a mattress. Nah, no cap, it wasn't me. Nah, yeah … I'll check, one sec.' He turned to me. 'Hey, Friar, What's your jefa's name?'

'Leonor González Rivera.'

'Leonor González Rivera, Boss … Yeah, that's it. No, um, couple of hours ago. Took her from El Peñón, yeah, Gloria Mendiola Road, that's the one, up on the hillside, right at the top.'

'It was patrol 4538-A,' I told him, just in case it was any help.

'Yeah, and the patrol number was …'

'4538-A.'

'4538-A … Bet. I'll call back later.'

Jeno put his phone away and said we could go, but I didn't want to. I preferred to wait my turn and speak to the lawyer. Jeno couldn't sit still. He stood up, he sat down, played with his phone, sent some messages, then he stood up again and said, 'I'll see you there. I'm gonna put some chilli in his tacos, you know, see if I can't speed him up some.'

'Hang on, yeah? Wait for me.'

'C'mon, I'm just trying to help. Relax, nothing's gonna happen and anyway, look how many people there are. Better off going to see the Boss. His office is somewhere around here.'

I thought about Miguel. How the hell could he have thought nicking a mattress was a good idea? When he started work at the factory, I thought he'd finally found something to stick at. After all, Má had asked him to find something stable. 'If you stay a bit longer, Miguel, they'll give you a bonus, insurance and all that,' she'd said.

Odd-jobbing was tough work and badly paid. I went along to help him once. We waited for ages at the San Pedro market 'til this one guy came along in this year's must-have pick-up. It was a Ford Lobo, black and beautiful with chrome hubcaps, like the ones the narcos have, and on the rear window, a Scarface sticker. Everyone knows that's the mark of the Zetas, same as the stickers with the skeleton figure of Our Lady of the Holy Death. Up on the hillside, on the footpaths, there was an altar dedicated to her, Our Lady of the Santa Muerte, because the Zetas consider her to be their patron saint. The altar was well tended with candles and everything. The first time I saw the altar it frightened me – a skeleton wearing a holy cape, her hands folded in prayer. And the candles, piles of candles, some lit, some not. Jeno would take offerings to her, I know that much.

As the truck pulled up in front of us, I felt scared. But they weren't narcos, or they didn't seem like it. The guy turned out to be pretty cool. He took us to a house in the Mitras district and told us to clear some of the rooms and put everything – bric-a-brac, old clothes, papers, the litter that had been collecting in the house – out on the roadside. A truck would stop by for it later. He was an analyst, or so he said when he caught me looking through some notebooks with strings of code written in them, like in the film *The Matrix*.

It was a large house with so many bedrooms, so many doors and windows, some big, some small, and it was a complete mess, but we did the job. It wasn't just debris we cleared – there were shedloads of clothes, old papers and several items of furniture that looked like they'd survived a flood. How could someone have so much stuff and just chuck it all out? It made me think of old Doña Lupita who used to push a supermarket trolley around the colonia collecting aluminium cans, pieces of wood and other bits and pieces. She'd pile them all up outside her house, either just to gather there or to re-sell the bottles and cans when she'd collected enough.

Miguel was in a good mood and wanted to stay in my good books – he'd only recently made up with Má after one of their arguments – but that positive energy only lasted until midday, and I spent the rest of the day doing the work for both of us. Around two o'clock the guy came back and brought us some pork tortas and fries that we devoured in seconds. I threw myself down on the ground in the shade of an alleyway to cool off while Miguel did the same in the patio. The smell of cigarette smoke wafted over, followed by a cough. We left around six and our sweaty bodies stank out the bus and its passengers. It was a huge job and all Miguel paid me was fifty pesos. He kept three hundred and fifty for himself. We'd never get rich like that.

Miguel had screwed us over. Who the hell would think to nick a mattress from a mattress factory, cart it through the city then drag it up a hill?

'Hey, Friar,' (that was Jeno's nickname for me because I never liked getting more involved in anything than was necessary. *With that attitude*, he said, *I'd never survive in the colonia*). 'I'm gonna take a leak, back soon.'

Jeno left and I was even more alone. I felt cold. The air con was on, or at least it was where I was sitting. It was blowing out from a vent just above my head and the breeze was blasting me, right down to my butt cheeks. I'd been worrying about Má, but now I began to think about Fredy and Marcos. I checked the clock on my phone. The afternoon had worn on and it was almost time for my brothers to come out of school. They'd be frightened if they arrived home to an empty house.

'Ninety-three,' muttered a man.

I went through to a desk where a Ministry man told me to sit down. I quickly explained what had happened and gave him Má's name. The man rifled through some files then typed something into the computer.

49

'Ah, yes. It says here she stole a mattress from the Súper Camas bed factory.'

'No, sir, no. The man who did it is Miguel Saldívar. He lives in the same colonia. It was him. That's who the cops came for, but they took my má instead.'

'Well, that's all well and good, kid, but where was the mattress? It says here it was found at the address stated, and it still had the plastic wrapping on it from the warehouse.'

'He took it there.'

'And he carried it there by himself, did he? I'm guessing he had some help, maybe even you, eh?'

I tensed and remained silent. I didn't want to end up in the slammer as well.

'I just want to know where my má is. It was patrol 4538-A that took her.'

The employee smiled sarcastically. 'What a kid, eh? You know everything about everything!'

The man typed some more things into his computer and eventually nodded. Then he called a young guy over and told him some details. The man set off through the desks and disappeared through a door. Ten minutes later he reappeared and handed a piece of paper to the man from the Ministry.

'OK, kiddo,' the man said eventually. 'It's a complicated one. They didn't bring your mamá here; they took her straight to the prison. Do you know where that is?'

I had no idea where it was, but I knew what the words meant: bail money. The impossible bail money. And if

I couldn't get it together pronto, they'd take her away from me.

'But I mean, why go around taking what isn't yours, chingados?' the man scolded me. 'That's all you people from the hillsides are good for.'

I left feeling gloomy.

My face hurt where the chota had hit me. It was as if someone had thrown me from the highest point of the house, off the cement roof of my beautiful home, down the hill where my head had landed in the pigsty muck, the rocks and the glass, the spit and shit of those who live on the hillside, the black streams of water that flow down the hill to the avenue at the bottom. Someone else had sent me reeling into some other pile – more dust, more glass – headlong into the waste that stuck to my armpits. My skin felt like the greasy paper they use to serve up beef tacos (if it really was beef) crossed with the shiny labels they stick on beer bottles and cleaning products. As I had rolled downhill, my fingers had felt the sharp edges of bottle caps and the spiky spines of bushes; my bones had rusted like the skywards-pointing rods poking out of the dozens of half-built houses; and my hair was a mane of cables and small strips of plastic from the bags of rubbish. By the time I had finally reached Eloy Cavazos Avenue, I had turned into one huge ball of garbage.

I left the Ministry building and headed to an open space to breathe in some air, as if all the buildings, cars and people had taken it away from me. I perched on the back of a bench. Poor Má, all alone in there, in the prison with rapists and thieves, sitting there next to killers and hitmen. Maybe that's where Don Neto had ended up – maybe he could help her? I could ask after him back in the colonia. Having a plan helped me to calm down … but then I remembered that favours don't come for free. Everything has a price.

I spotted Jeno smoking, and he had some good news: we could go and see the Boss. There was still a little part of me, a small scrap of skin hanging in there with something to offer.

We walked to the lawyer's office. It wasn't far from the ministerio público, located in a narrow five-storey building with an old lift that whirred past each floor. We went up to the top floor and along an endless corridor of metal doors showing the names of the lawyers, doctors and dentists who worked there.

Jeno knocked at the next to last office, a sign on the door announced *Criminal Lawyer, Raúl Morcillo Bautista*. The door opened and we were ushered in by a girl who must have been about eighteen years old. Jeno went over and cheerfully said hi. She was of average height, curly hair down to her shoulders, white skin, small eyes and pink lips. She was wearing a white shirt and jeans with some colourful bracelets. I'd never seen a girl as pretty as her before. She was so pretty I felt a knot form in my throat and for a few moments, I forgot everything.

'We're here to see the Boss,' announced Jeno confidently. 'Friar, this is Estrella, Señor Raúl's niece.'

I approached her all starry-eyed and extended my hand. Estrella gave a little wave before she eventually took it. As I squeezed her hand, I came over all weird. Her palm was smooth and warm, but not sweaty. It was soft and hot. I don't know how to describe it; it was like squeezing a sponge. But then I saw myself through her eyes: skinny, undernourished, sweaty, with a massive T-shirt, short hair and worn-out shoes.

She didn't look like anyone from our colonia, at least none of the girls I knew. In the second year at high school, I'd had a girlfriend called Irma. She was kind of skinny, but her mouth and her voice drove me crazy. We went out for a few months and we made out like everyone else up there on the hillside. Sometimes we went to eat some elotes downtown, hanging out in Morelos Square, before coming back to the hill at night. She wanted to study to become a nurse. We went out until she moved away. I didn't like her old man though; he was a drunk. Once he yelled at her in front of me and I tried to defend her, but it was impossible. Even so, we can't have liked each other that much because once she'd moved away, we didn't even try to meet up again. Irma had been my first girlfriend and afterwards, at the parties in some of the other colonias, I'd get off with some girl or other, but it never went any further and I didn't ever push it. Like I was still getting over her or something.

Estrella, though, she was on another level.

'He won't be long. Wait there.' She gestured to a couple of seats.

We sat down, but I couldn't keep my eyes off her. Her curly hair looked fresh and natural, unlike the girls from our colonia who always wore it choppy and dyed with different coloured streaks. Estrella shuffled some papers then looked at files on the computer screen in front of her.

It was only a few minutes before we heard the main door creak open and the Boss walked in. He greeted Jeno and waved us through into his office. He kissed his niece on the cheek and, following us in, put his rucksack down on a chair. He didn't dress like a lawyer; he was wearing a grey shirt tucked into jeans with white sports shoes. What surprised me most, though, was his face. He looked so young, too young; I'm not sure I can explain it. He must have been about forty, but he looked at least ten years younger. I don't know why, but that fact somehow gave me confidence; however, all that disappeared as soon as he said he'd been doing some digging, and he didn't have good news for me.

'You see, the thing is, this factory they stole the mattress from always goes on the attack. Their lawyer handed over some extra cash, that's why they took her straight to the prison. I've seen cases like this before. They're super quick and always end badly. What we need to do now is submit a series of amparos to halt proceedings.' I tried to follow what he was saying, but the Boss noticed I was a bit lost, so he added, 'Let me explain. So, Friar … what's your real name? Efraín? OK, Efraín, they've taken your mamá straight to the prison. And look, chamaco, they're not particularly bothered whether your mamá is guilty or innocent. They'll go up against anyone, as long as they can use it to teach someone a lesson. At least they're not accusing you of anything worse.'

'But it was Miguel, Má's partner.'

'I don't mean to sound rude, but they really don't care who *actually* did it. They're not even out there looking for this Miguel fella. And the case will cost. I'll help you but I have to involve the State Commission for Human Rights because of how unwarranted it all was: entering the premises without any sort of judicial warrant, arresting a third person under threat of violence. But the problem is, she's already inside and the system's in a big ol' mess because they cut the Commission's budget by more than half due to "austerity". As I say, the real problem is, they've already put her away.'

I felt the disappointment crushing my throat.

'What are those bruises?' the Boss asked me.

'The chotas.'

'Let me take some photos.'

He took out his phone and snapped some pictures, zooming in for some close-ups.

'These people don't believe in justice. Sometimes I get it, you know, living surrounded by violence and corruption all the time hardens them to it. Right, I'm going to file a complaint because of that beating. Here's my phone number. I'll investigate but I'll need some cash. If it helps, think of it as a symbolic payment, but I can't do anything without the first transaction. That's my rule. You get nothing for nothing, but everything comes with a discount. Look, the money isn't even for me. It's for my contacts inside, to find out more. Go get the cash and I'll start making my moves tomorrow.'

'Not 'til tomorrow?'

The Boss gestured for me to calm down. 'I know, I know, every minute feels like an age for you right now, but there's nothing else I can do today. She'll be all right inside and they don't share cells. She'll be there another two or three days before they transfer her, which will give us time to make our move. But I need that money. And after that, I'll need some more. Justice will come, but it'll come faster with money.'

'Aren't there any of those defence lawyers, the ones who don't charge anything?'

'What do you think I am, hey, kid?' Raúl turned to look at Jeno. 'Look, Efraín, I'll go over it one more time for you. Inside everything is *money, money, money*. If you don't believe me, ask your buddy Jeno here.'

I turned to look at my friend who nodded.

'But I don't have any.'

'Look, chamaco. I'm going to tell it to you straight because this is the only way you'll understand: the cops and the lawyers in there don't care. Your mamá is just another number to them, and one that they can use to get money out of. That's their real job – not seeking justice but getting money out of someone accused of being a thief, a murderer, a rapist, a conman, take your pick. Put your batteries in, find the dough and bring it to the prison tomorrow. And then we can reassure your mamá that someone will take care of her legally.'

I was silent, thinking about my brothers. Then, 'Can't you go now? Má must be worried.'

The Boss smiled. 'No, Efraín, I can't go now, but I will do something for you, just so you believe me, OK?' And saying that, he took out his phone and dialled a number. He stood up, maybe to make himself feel important or something. He smiled and greeted the person on the other end of the line. They exchanged a couple of jokes before the Boss mentioned Má's name and added, 'Tell her I'll be defending her, and that I spoke to her son ...' And, turning to me, he asked, 'What are your names, you and your brothers?' I stammered my answer. Raúl repeated my words, but it was like hearing them far away in the distance, words with no meaning, weightless, soulless words that had escaped from my mouth. Something in my brain had turned off. It was the anxiety, stretching, becoming long and thin, very long, as long as the roads from here to the colonia. 'Great, perfect,' Raúl said finally. He made another joke, laughed and ended the call. 'Well, Efraín, that's settled. Get the money for tomorrow. Now, scram. I've got other clients to see. But don't worry. We'll get her out.'

'But how much?'

'Five. That'll do as a starter.'

Five thousand! A whole month's wages for Má. A huge amount of money. When we left, it was almost evening. Estrella had already finished and gone. Jeno still had some cash left from the money he'd stolen from the driver, so we stopped at a taco stand on the way home. My senses were playing tricks because while the meat cooking on the grill smelled incredible, with the potatoes and fried onions, the first bite tasted like paper in my mouth. Jeno gave me some money to take home a couple of portions for my brothers and he handed over another couple of two-hundred-peso notes.

'S'not much, but money comes, money goes. Take what's left to help with what you need for your jefa. You scratch my back, I'll scratch yours. I mean, there's so many wallets out there in people's pockets, they make it easy for us!'

We headed up Montes Azules Road and when we reached El Rancho, Jeno veered off to hang out with some other guys while I continued my journey home alone. As we went our separate ways, he checked again, 'All good now, yeah?'

'Getting there.'

Jeno turned back to his gang before adding, 'If you like, I can ask around, see if anyone's got any contacts inside to help your jefa. We've got loads of guys down there. But you know it don't come free. Lemme know, yeah?'

I hesitated. Jeno had been a lookout for Don Neto and sometimes he'd passed goods across the city in taxis. I knew some of the others who were mixed up with that sort of stuff, some on the outside, a lot on the inside, most already dead or disappeared, but he was right. You had to pay for help on the inside – it made your stay much easier. Even so, I didn't hesitate long.

'No. Leave it for now. See what the Boss has to say.'

I walked up to the house in silence. From the neighbouring houses floated sounds from TVs and radios. A pig squealed somewhere down below. The wind picked up. I looked out over the city, already enveloped by the night. I felt eyes watching me. In the distance, towards the airport, immense warehouses rose up, part of a factory I'd never seen close up. The car headlights on the far-off avenues came and went as always. Far beyond that, the flames from the chimneys of the Cadereyta refinery floated in the darkness. I found Fredy and Marcos waiting for me at home, dressed only in shorts. I'd forgotten they had a key. The heat of the day was only now starting to drop.

'Má?' asked Marcos, sounding hopeful that she might be following behind me.

I shook my head.

'S'true then?' asked Fredy.

'Yep.'

Marcos started crying and I let him – why try and stop him doing exactly what I'd been wanting to do since the moment they took her away? When they got home from school, some of the women nearby had told them what had happened, so they weren't surprised to find the house destroyed and in darkness.

I asked them if they'd seen Miguel. Apparently someone had seen him legging it from Israel's store when he heard the feds had taken Má.

'The old jerk,' I swore. 'Well, I've got a lawyer. You'd better eat and we'll see what happens. We'll get Má out, you'll see.'

I handed over the bags with the tacos and my brothers sat on the floor to eat. They'd made a start on clearing up the mess the police had left. I thought about Estrella.

We have a torch we use when there's someone stirring the devils down below and we need to keep the lights off. I picked it up now and headed out along a route that only Má and I know. Up above, the sound of the crickets, the wings of some nocturnal bird and the wind hissed in my ears. Down below, the city had been swallowed by lights, a mass of blinking dots. I finally found what I was looking for: a group of three medium-sized flat stones, piled one on top of the other, as if left there by time and the hillside itself. I sat down and started digging off to one side. It wasn't long before I hit the Cloralex tub covered with the rubber from a burst balloon. I unwrapped it and took out the money.

The notes were all rolled up: Má's savings, and mine from the jobs I'd done. I counted the money: sixteen thousand six hundred pesos. I took what I needed to complete the five thousand, and a little more for what we needed, before burying the tub again, this time a little further away from the stones.

As I returned down the path, a cold and very strong gust of wind almost lifted my feet from the ground, but I clung to some nearby bushes. Sometimes the wind blows so hard it takes the corrugated metal roofs off the houses below, and occasionally even some of the hens lift off, along with T-shirts, trousers and socks, all gliding uphill in the gusts. Whenever that happens, I imagine falling off the hillside and floating up towards the heavens while I watch everything else left behind. When you live so high up, it's easy to dream of flying.

When I got home, I heard Fredy telling Marcos he'd do whatever he had to get Má out of jail, that if they gave him a gun, he'd go in and get her, rescuing her while under fire. Marcos listened to him attentively. In a house further down, they had a stereo turned up loud. When I heard the music, the words singing about smoke, I felt like it was me that had been turned to smoke, a black fog that danced among the roofs of the homes around me.

7

I couldn't sleep because my face was hurting, and I didn't have any painkillers.

I went outside and sat on the square rock next to the door. Who knew when the rock first broke off from the hillside, sitting there for years, existing as nothing more than a boulder until the day Papá decided to use it. Above the city, on the summits of the nearby mountains, the clouds were stretched like cigars. The night was painted a dark blue. 'Think, Efraín, think,' I said to myself. I made a plan. I had no idea how things stood in the local prison, but I knew conditions would be better there than in the federal one. Some of the neighbours had spent time in both places and always spoke better of the local one, common knowledge.

The cells, the prison, the jail, the correctional. Jeno was like so many others – Rulo, Sanchís, Parca, Mole, El Turu. It was the done thing: go in, come out, head back to school, even if they'd fallen behind a year. Almost all of them smoked weed, some did snow, then they'd take refuge in some rehab place, celebrating keeping clean for a while. They'd set themselves up selling tacos at the crossroads to try and earn some money. Sometime later, they'd fall off the wagon and the cycle would start again.

Or at least it did 'til they stopped going to rehab after some incident where the Zetas went after some guy who was in there (God knows what he'd done). They got in and shot the lot. That's where they'd killed Javo, second-in-command to Don Neto. Loads more too.

During the times of la lumbre, the big narco wars, every two or three days we'd hear something new. They killed Luisfe in Eloy Cavazos Avenue outside a hardware store. They got the girls Lupe and Telma at home, they even did their grandparents. They smoked Crazy Carlos (I went through primary school with him) and one day his body just appeared, dumped on a bench, like it was nothing. Without any shoes. I always wondered why they took people's shoes, although deep down I knew. It was a warning: you can't run.

The lucky ones moved to other colonias, or their mamás sent them back to the villages they came from, or they were so little involved in what was going on that nobody paid them any attention because they knew nothing. Or they were forced to sign up, like Jeno. And then there were others they left out of it completely, maybe because they smelled that we didn't have the desire or the strength to get involved. A pick-up never came to find me during the night with a task, or to offer me a job. For us, it was school then home, followed by homework and chores. Maybe it would all have been different if I'd have been fifteen back then. But we were Leonor's sons and we were lucky. It was that simple.

With the older guys it was different. At school we'd get together to chat during break and tell stories about the neighbourhood narcos. Some of the others even had videos of people they'd tortured, but not all of us could bear to watch. It was better just to leave. Those guys went straight from the classroom door to the pick-ups waiting outside to exchange money for goods; there was a pusher in the classroom selling mostly weed in small plastic bags. We always lived on the edge of the law, or just next to it, like one of the streams of water that flows down the hillside when it rains. You heard all these stories, you grew up with them, alongside the certainty that you have to do something really bad to end up rotting in jail. Miguel told us some of those stories too. I should have realised right there and then he wasn't to be trusted – you always try to copy what you admire. But he wasn't a narco, or a big-time thief, just some dopey old mattress stealer. It was laughable really.

But with Má it was different.

She once took us to a very large house where they paid her well to clean. Your jaw dropped right from the moment you stepped into the kitchen: a cooker with six burners; a fridge with two doors, gleaming like glass; a huge store cupboard filled with various brands of biscuits, bags of tostadas, Frosties, Choco Krispies and other sweet treats.

Má ordered us to stay in the kitchen and not to wander around the rest of the house or go anywhere else until she'd finished, as if us just walking around the rooms was bad. Anyway, the house was empty – the owners were out at work during the day – and the only thing in the massive garage was the sunshine. Fredy and Marcos must have been about nine and seven and Má had made it easy for them. She sent me off to a shop miles away to buy some cans of cola for lunch. The owner had given her permission to take food from the fridge, but she didn't want to; if you took one thing, for some people it would only take a small leap to accuse you of theft. It was better not to feed suspicions like that.

I felt eyes watching me the whole way there, but differently from when I'm on the hillside. Up there they're watching to see if you're carrying anything of value, or to see who you're with. Here it was different: *I* was the danger. I caught sight of my reflection in a car window and felt far removed from that neighbourhood with the big houses, the gardens with immense, well-pruned trees, the walls and fences topped with security cameras. It was like being in a magazine about mansions, one of those grubby old mags you'd find for sale at the flea market on Montes Azules Road.

A guy guarding one of the houses watched me as I went past, he even picked up his walkie-talkie to call someone.

I'd never seen so many security cameras as I did that day. Since then, I've felt like there's a camera trained on me, watching my every step whenever I enter one of those neighbourhoods, another when people bump into me in the shopping centre and think I'm going to mug them, another when I walk near someone well-dressed in a jacket and jewels and they sense me nearby, crossing the road so I don't follow them. I'm watched the whole time. When we're out as a group, mostly nothing happens. We hide, we play, we mess about, we laugh, we go wherever we like and people leave us alone. But when we go to the mall on our own, or we start walking towards a shop, we know we're under observation. Sometimes when I go to Walmart with Jeno, I check. The eyes of the security guard watch us, the check-out assistants, the women shopping wait for us to kick off, a pack of security cameras sniffs us out and follows us. Some people, like Jeno, aren't bothered by it – they walk around sticking their hands into whatever they fancy like nothing's going on. But other people, like me, prefer to glue our arms by our sides so no one has a chance to accuse us of anything.

And with that feeling of being watched, I returned with the cans and found Má cleaning the garage. I walked into the kitchen but couldn't see my brothers. I started to search for them. The house had so many rooms, spread across different floors. There was even a library with several paintings hanging on the walls. And the books! I'd never seen so many. I mean, of course, I'd seen the ones at school at the beginning of each year, but in this house there were so, so many, all organised by colour. One lay on a table in the middle of the room. It was huge and the title read *Great Discoverers and Conquerors*. I didn't dare open it, but it looked fascinating. There were lots of pieces of wooden furniture, pictures and miniature soldiers. In the living room – spotless – I braved sitting on one of the leather chairs. I walked along a corridor and checked behind several doors, but no luck. I finally found my brothers in a storage room at the back of the house, full of boxes, tools and a jumble of other bits and pieces. Then I heard the crunch. They were eating biscuits.

'What the—?!' I swore at them. 'You idiots! What are you doing back here? What if the owners come back?'

My brothers jumped out of their skins. They'd been on high alert since sneaking out of the kitchen.

'Where d'you get those?'

Admittedly, they looked amazing: chocolate-covered marshmallows sitting on a biscuit base with strawberry pieces sprinkled on top.

'They were just there.'

On a table, I discovered a packet with ripped packaging. I read the name of the brand and started to drag my brothers back to the kitchen, but Má was waiting for us in the corridor. When she saw us, Má turned red with anger and embarrassment, or perhaps something else I didn't recognise.

'Where have you been?'

Fredy hid the food and Marcos copied him, but not quite as well. Má stormed over and ordered him to show her his hands. When she found the biscuits, I saw the horror in her eyes.

'Who told you that you could take what isn't yours?' The expression on Má's face said it all.

When Má beat you, she did it well. She used to whip me with whatever she had to hand, even using twigs from the bushes on the hillside, but since Papá had died, she'd stopped.

'Hands out,' she commanded.

'It was only one,' said Fredy.

'No, Mamá, no,' whimpered Marcos.

They knew the punishment.

'Don't even think about crying.'

The slaps rained down on their hands carrying all the rage Má felt. My brothers turned red from the pain before the fear paled their cheeks. On the floor lay biscuit crumbs.

'You kids have no idea what trust means to these people. We are their servants, even if they don't call us that. We are their servants, even if they give us a lift somewhere, or they give us presents, even if we look after their children or we make food for them. We are nothing but their servants.'

At the time, I had no idea what Má was talking about, much less my brothers, but a long time later it started to make sense and I have since come to understand. It's simple really. I've accepted it. Some people are here, others are there, and some of us try to make it between the two as best we can.

'I saw biscuits like that in the store,' I told her to help calm her down.

Her eyes opened wide with relief. 'Go and buy some, mijo,' she said quickly, taking out a couple of coins from her pocket. 'Go, quickly. The owner will be back soon. He always comes home for lunch.'

I flew to the store. Every car that passed me was the owner's. 'Don't run,' I told myself, but even so, I sped there, bought the biscuits and got back just as the owner arrived home. He looked me up and down from top to bottom, surprised to see me wandering into his house so freely.

'Are you Leonor's son?' he asked, concern visible on his face.

I nodded.

'You scared me,' and then he smiled. 'Do you know if your mamá made lunch yet? I'm in a hurry so I'm flying in and out.'

I nodded again.

The owner went inside while I stayed in the garage. The sun warmed my legs. I stayed there, expecting the worst. My hands melted the biscuits in their packet. I've never known if Má was exaggerating. I was about to move when the owner came out again holding a plastic tub. He stood watching me for a moment before climbing into his car.

'Can I go now?' he asked, amused, and when I glanced at the tub, he thought he needed to explain. 'Eating at home is better ... but when you've got things to do ...'

I stepped to one side. The guy gave a last smile and left. When I got inside, Má was washing dirty plates.

'What happened?'

'Did you buy them?'

I showed her the packet.

'Give them to me.'

Fredy and Marcos were near the fridge, they'd been crying. Má shot them a look of annoyance. The punishment hadn't finished yet. She sat down at the table, opened the packet, took out a biscuit and calmly ate it, followed by the next. She sat there and ate them all, one at a time.

'In this family, we do not steal,' she pronounced.

Later my brothers told me that while she had been serving the man his lunch, Má had handed him some coins. The owner seemed confused, and she confessed that her kids had eaten some biscuits and she'd prefer to just come clean so he could decide whether her services were still required. The owner's thoughts had been miles away. He looked out the window and asked why I was outside. In the end, he smiled and told Má she needn't worry. 'Thanks for telling me, but they're only biscuits and you know you're welcome to eat anything here – you and your children. Just let me know what you've had. I've got to run. I'll leave the money for the electricity and telephone here. Buy yourself and the boys some biscuits with the change.'

Má paid the electricity and the phone bill but didn't buy us anything.

On the way home, Fredy had grumbled, 'She's so over the top. It was just some stupid cookies. Next time I'm going to grab the whole lot and cram them in my face. Did you see all the stuff in that house? They don't even know they've got half of it.'

'The day she finds out, she'll throw you out,' I warned him.

'Nah, she won't know … I go with Luisfe and the others. We go to the Oxxo store down on the avenue and nick stuff. They've not caught us yet,' he confessed.

'Well, you do that if you want to, but just don't get Marcos involved, yeah?'

Má never took us to any of the houses where she worked again. It was a pity; I'd never seen such beautiful places, both inside and out. Just looking at those interiors, the furniture, the accessories and the paintings was stealing.

That first night without Má I had a bitter taste in my mouth. How I wished I had a chocolate biscuit to take away the sour saliva that burned beneath my tongue. Just as I was dropping off, I heard a bark up at the top of the mountain where a TV antenna blinked. It was a dry bark, almost a howl, or maybe it was a lament. Or perhaps it was a gunshot, an execution. It wouldn't be the first time. The hillside was covered with graves and bodies, with ghosts clamouring for the justice nobody ever granted. A shiver ran down my neck as I sensed something moving in the darkness. Better to stay inside. It was probably just the wind … or perhaps it was someone heading to the altar of the Santa Muerte – the Holy Death – to leave an offering in the dead of night.

8

I didn't go to school that morning, but I told my brothers to go to class if I wasn't back by one. At first, they didn't want to go, but they ended up doing it anyway. Fredy told me he could start working, doing whatever he needed to do to get the cash for the lawyer.

'No,' I replied. 'I'll sort it.'

I had decided to be like Má and try to think things through the way she would've wanted. What would she have done in my place? First off, she'd have done everything she could to get everything back to normal. There wasn't anything for breakfast, so I headed off with an empty belly, but I left my brothers some money so they could buy something to eat.

Before I reached the avenue, I stopped off at Miguel's. I knocked and knocked on the corrugated door, but nobody answered it. That house was always full of people – about fifteen people lived there – but nobody came out. I'd find him.

Down on the avenue, at the bus stop under the footbridge, I saw El Turu selling newspapers. For a while, I'd helped him with deliveries, but you didn't earn very much. He asked me if I'd left school and I told him no, I was just on an errand. 'A'right,' he replied. My bus was nearly there so I said goodbye and climbed on board. There were no seats, so I stood on the steps by the back door, one foot on the step, the other in mid-air. My tummy rumbled and I kept one hand in my trouser pocket to stroke the notes.

Five thousand pesos was a lot! With five thousand pesos we could buy like two hundred and forty litres of milk, or a hundred and sixty caguamas of beer, or two hundred and fifty kilos of tortillas. We could live off it for months eating nothing but frijoles and bread, or we could play video games at Isra's for two hundred hours. We could buy eighty portions of tacos de barbacoa on Sundays, or two hundred DVDs, or fifty chickens to roast, or twenty pairs of new trainers at the market.

If I had five thousand pesos to use just for me, I'd buy a load of oranges and then I'd sell them. With the money from selling the oranges, I'd buy twice as many, and I'd sell them all again. Then with that money, I'd buy a cart to take around the streets and sell oranges to more people, and with that money, I'd save up to get a little stand, something simple, but a stand all the same, next to the bus stop, with a blender – just one – so I could sell smoothies and juices. And with the money from those juices and smoothies, I could buy more blenders, hire another kid from El Peñón, and put up another stand at another bus stop. I could do a lot with five thousand pesos, and I rubbed the edges of the notes. Daydreaming about all that, I'd forgotten it wasn't even mine and would never serve to start a business.

I sighed and concentrated on the packed bus. Just as we were leaving Guadalupe district, a space opened in the seats at the back and I sat down, squeezed up against the window next to an older guy – he must have been about forty-five – with very red skin and a flat nose. In his lap he had a toolbox, perhaps he was an electrician. I felt like I recognised his face, but I couldn't place him. At this time of the day there were lots of men like him with the tools of their trades in plastic tubs or boxes: tilers with their cutting tools, electricians with their pliers, road workers with their gauges and spirit levels. A few of them though, just had their hands, like Miguel.

The idea crept up on me: I ought to find an actual job and save money for the lawyer. But where could I work and how much would they pay me? Perhaps I could approach the ladies Má used to clean for, but it wasn't like they would actually want to hire me, and anyway, I knew how to wash and iron but that was about it. Besides, they'd never trust me. And I wasn't about to tell them Má was in prison. Thinking along those lines, I came up with an elaborate plan to tell them she couldn't come to work because a relative had fallen sick back in her village, that much could've been true. Má hadn't been born up here in Monterrey, but in a little village north of Veracruz. She'd come up here with Papá. We'd been born here though, in the Gine hospital, she'd told us once.

Sometimes I wonder what our lives might have been like if we'd have stayed down there in the village. Would our tastes or ways of thinking be different? Would different things make us happy or annoy us? Would we meet people from the city, look down our noses and laugh at them, because, poor things, they were all locked up, squeezed together with no space to breathe and more roads than houses? Má would have a stand selling delicious home-made gorditas and picadas, and Papá would still be a labourer, like my grandparents who grew soya until they lost their land.

I got off the bus in the city centre and walked the many streets to get to Raúl's office. Next to the main entrance, a man was selling cold tortas, they looked so good, bread rolls filled with ham, cheese and avocado. This time I climbed the stairs because I didn't quite trust the lift. Secretly I hoped to see Estrella, but when I knocked on the door and it opened, an older lady appeared, smelling of Vicks Vaporub. She was fat, a double chin hanging off the bottom of her face, and she had a small phone pressed to her ear.

'I'm looking for Señor Raúl.'

'Are you Efraín Martínez?'

I nodded.

'Señor Morcillo isn't going to be in until later on, but he told me to expect you. You can call him later. Here's your receipt.'

'But he told me he'd be here.'

'Well yes, but he had a call from the Ministry.'

'Are you his secretary? Only there was another girl here yesterday.'

'The skinny girl with the curly hair?'

'Yeah.'

'That's his niece, she helps out sometimes, but I'm Señor Morcillo's assistant. Anything else?'

'No, just … when is she in?'

'Some days she works, some days she doesn't. Señor Morcillo is helping to pay for her school.'

We're not that different then, I thought. I really didn't want to hand the money over to the new lady, but she was determined, like so many of the women back home in the colonia. Big women, made on the streets, with powerful voices, impulsive, ready to haggle, jefas in the full meaning of the word – they were definitely in charge. Women who would do whatever it took to provide money and food for their families. Sometimes there'd be a fight and the older boys would watch the women grab hold of each other in the street and follow them to wherever they ended up, until they were pulled apart, usually by some other women or their kids.

'And, what was your name, ma'am?'

'You can call me Señora Maribel.'

I handed over the money. There was no other option.

'Call him later on. Señor Morcillo will tell you what to do.'

'Where's the prison?'

'There are three of them but let me see if Señor Morcillo made a note of where your jefa is.'

The woman went into the office and when she came back, she handed me a note with tiny blue writing on it.

'She's in the one down in Venustiano, but they won't let you in.'

When I left the office, it was already past ten o'clock. I was really hungry and thirsty by now. Downstairs I hung around on the roadside without a clue as to where to go. Back home? Or see if they'd let me in at school? Or go and look for work? I sat down on the walkway and people-watched. They came and went. Some were absent-minded, seemingly on holiday or with no need to rush. Others walked by quickly. The leisurely ones stopped to look in the windows, the hasty ones walked with their heads up high, locomotives of flesh and bone ready to barge anyone who crossed their path out of the way. My insides groaned. Behind me, the sandwiches the man was selling called to me, that and a really cold can of cola.

I started walking to the jail. I was starving, so as I walked I counted the number of food stalls or restaurants: four taco stands, one Quesadillas México outlet, one trader selling spicy tortas, one KFC, one McDonald's, one man selling hot churros in paper bags, one Michoacana ice cream stall, one juice bar. Further on I came across a pizzeria shrouded in its aroma of baked dough and tomato sauce, followed by many streets absent of flavours and aromas, until I finally reached another fried quesadilla place and two taco stands clouded in steam. The street food was such a temptation.

Eventually I got to the prison. It was still officially the city centre, but the houses around here were much bigger. The building itself stood out because it was the only one that looked like a cube of cement with a huge grey gate. That, and because there were several patrol cars and riot vans parked outside. A man under a tree was selling jicamas, pineapples and tuna fruits from a cart. There were more people hovering around. All of them with their eyes on the doors of the law. Two female police officers and two other guards waited outside, armed with machine guns.

I waited in the shade unsure whether to approach one of the officers; the women seemed a safer bet. All police officers screw you around – they shout at you and beat you – but when it's a woman, it's more like being told off by your má, your grandma, your aunties, your great-grandma, or another woman like that. It's enough for one woman to have a go at you for her to be speaking on behalf of all the women in the world, that punishing tone, at pains to make sure you understand because the world isn't made for messing around. Or at least that's how it was when Má had a go at me.

I plucked up my courage and approached one of the policewomen who looked me up and down. I asked after Má, stating her full name. All I wanted was to check she was definitely there. The woman neither confirmed nor denied it.

'It's only the lawyers who come in here, chamaco. And we only give information to the lawyers. You got one of those yet?'

'Yeah.'

The woman looked surprised. 'Like I say, I can't tell you any more. Now disappear before the guards up there start shooting.'

I looked towards a wide house and spotted a couple of officers wearing protective black helmets and bullet-proof vests. One kept his eyes on me the whole time.

'It's a lady who came in for stealing a mattress … but she's innocent, I swear.'

The woman smiled. 'I can't tell you anything, but I have seen them bring people in because they've stolen mattresses, that's all I'll say. Now, you little wart, go and find your lawyer.'

When I got home, my brothers had already left for school. I spent the rest of the afternoon mulling over what to do. I went to look for Miguel again, but the house was still shut up so I went to hang out with Jeno who was down at El Rancho listening to some tunes by Cartel de Santa. That's where my brothers found me, and we walked back up the hillside together.

'Did you see her?' Fredy asked.

'No, but I checked where they've got her.'

'Can we go visit?'

'Don't think so.'

I was explaining what I'd done when the Boss's call came through.

'I've started a writ of amparo but just doing that used up nearly all the five thousand you gave me. We'll need more. I managed to get them to hold your jefa where she is for a few more days before they move her to the women's prison. And the news from the Commission is that they want to take on your má's case, but they haven't confirmed it yet. I'll keep chasing.'

I froze. They were going to lock her up already? For a mattress she hadn't even stolen?

'How much more do you need?'

'Another four thousand, for the amparo and other paperwork.'

'I'll bring it tomorrow.'

As I ended the call, I felt my knees buckle like they were useless, but I thought I needed to show I was being strong, so I pulled myself together.

'What did he say?' asked Fredy.

'He wants more money.'

'And do we have it?'

'It'll come from somewhere. Miguel's family'll probably help us,' I said, just to say something really, although it wasn't such a bad idea.

9

We went to see whether he'd grown the balls to own up to what he'd done.

Pinche Miguel!

Má had met him the same way you meet everyone here: coming and going in the street. Miguel had seen her one afternoon on her way back from work. Má was carrying some food home, her bag split and Miguel saw his chance. He went over and helped. Má's not one of those who is easily swayed so God knows why she let him help. Perhaps it was just one of those days where you're so, so tired you just want everything to be done already. I say that cos that's how I feel sometimes, like I just want to leave this place and live in a big house with a car.

Miguel accompanied her as far as El Rancho and they said goodbye. But he knew where to find her, and a few weeks later, that's exactly what happened. One afternoon, he invited her to dinner at one of the burger joints down on the avenue – Tío's – the sort of place loads of people go. Má didn't accept the invitation, but they kept bumping into each other, on the road, at the bus stop. And after about a year of chasing after her, Miguel arrived at the house and Má presented him as her boyfriend. He's been hanging around here ever since.

The next day was Saturday and we went down to the flea market. We were fooling around down there until Fredy suggested we try Miguel's and see if anyone was around. His brothers were there, the ones who'd helped us with the mattress. They were sitting around outside in some rocking chairs, caguamas at their feet. From inside the house floated an old norteña song about a schoolteacher turned assassin. I asked after Miguel, but the brothers hadn't seen him since the weekend they helped us. One of them picked up a beer and took a swig, then he blew his nose and spat off to one side. They were playing cards. I asked them where else he could be, where he might be hiding, and one of the other brothers laughed.

'Ha! He's probably somewhere sleeping off one of his benders,' another brother laughed.

One of them, the one who looked the oldest, eventually asked, 'How's your jefa, your má?'

I didn't know how to answer. Why repeat what they already knew?

'They're probably going to send her down.'

The man shook his head. 'Pinche Miguel,' he swore. 'He's always been good at screwing up the lives of everyone around him.'

'Can you help us find him?'

The brother squirmed uncomfortably. Just then, their mamá came out the house. She was a woman showing her age, with wrinkles and grey hair. She was short, with a large belly and a mole on one of her eyelids. She was wearing a red flowery dress and glasses.

'Leonor's kids,' said the one who'd asked after Má.

The woman's eyes swept over us. Her expression was one of anger, or perhaps irritation. She asked one of her sons for a beer and took a sip, barely a mouthful, just to put some distance between us. I looked at my brothers who were watching the scene, clueless as to what to do.

'Shouldn't you be working?' she asked one of her sons.

'It's Saturday, jefa, and anyway, the part we need hasn't arrived.'

'Well, go and get it then, that's what your feet are for. And you? Haven't you got a delivery for Susana?'

'Yes, jefa.'

'So what are you lazing around here with your brothers for then? What 'bout you, Chava?'

'Day off, jefa.'

'Find me a chair.'

They pulled over a seat next to them. Neither the brother who ought to go to the workshop nor the one with the delivery for Susana stood up to go. The señora sat watching us and eventually grimaced in resignation.

'My Miguel's the middle one, he's always been a bit slow. When he was a little boy, he once ran away from school, he'd only just turned six. He was just wandering round, not thinking about what he was doing and ended up stuck on top of the fence he was trying to climb over. There he was, crying and crying 'til the teacher went to get him. And then she called me. I gave him what for …'

Miguel's brothers smiled at that.

'He didn't even finish high school because he went off to work with his papá. It was all going well, and he was earning good money, not that it helped him much. After that he got married, divorced and they took his girls away. Then he got together with Luisa, before breaking up with her. He's not a bad man, just a fool. I don't know any mother who'd want stupid or lazy children, but it don't make a difference whether you want them or not. I mean, look how mine turned out.'

The woman's sons started to squirm in their chairs, embarrassed.

'See, thing is, who knows where my son is right now? And what exactly do you want by coming here? Even if he does show up, how we gonna make him turn himself in? Who's gonna tell him to stop roaming and put himself in jail for a year or two? Just so they can rough him up? All for nothing.'

The woman shook her head.

'Ah, Miguel, the damn fool! He may be my son, but still, you don't deserve to be without a mother. We'll see if we can find him for you. I've been thinking about it, and I said to myself, "If they come here, I'll help them". And that's what I'm gonna do, just don't come back. You know how it goes, we've all gotta get by as best we can.'

And saying that, she held out a piece of paper. On it were the names of several business, workshops and car garages, the names of bars Miguel drank in, a couple of factories and a discount store. That was all we were going to get out of them. I said thanks, but what I really wanted to do was roar at the woman. I gathered up my little brothers and we turned to go. Behind us the men carried on drinking.

'We ought to do her house over,' muttered Fredy, who was doing all he could not to pick up a stone and throw it at them. 'That ugly old bag, and Má in jail. What's on the paper?'

'Think it's all the places where Miguel's been working.'

'Pfff, how's that gonna help us?'

'Maybe they'll know where he is.'

'Don't think so. I reckon we ought to ask Jeno. He's got loads of different ways to help, of finding Miguel for us,' announced Fredy. 'You're just not on it, Efra.'

For his twelve years, he had a rebellious look about him, I could see it. He'd grown taller than I'd realised, and his head was shaved because that was the done thing round here, to have it almost right down to the skin, but not like a military buzzcut, it was a different style. Everyone went to the Kolombias' place for their hair because no one else did it the same. Some of the skatos – the ska kids – went elsewhere, but the Kolombias were the best. First they'd rub a wet towel over your head, then they'd cover your neck with a cloth and brush through the long sections at the front, snip, snip, brush, snip, clippers on a number two, brush, snip, brush, snip, sideburns, razor round the back, long strokes, talc on the ears. Then we'd go and hang out down at the video games to show off the fresh trim, or head over to Riri's, who sold spliffs alongside his tacos (for local consumption rather than the guys who came every so often for a dose of something stronger from Jeno).

'Don't even think about it. If we get mixed up in that, we'll never get out of it again,' I warned my brother.

We went back round the corner and sat outside a store to think through our next steps. I had some money left over so we went back to the market and picked up some tacos from one of the stands. They submerged the beef in the hot oil, golden onions floating around the edges. We ordered three portions, bought some cola and went to sit down on the floor nearby. The old woman was right: we had to get by the best we could, and Leonor's sons were *not* going to be like hers.

Once we had finished, I explained to my brothers that if Miguel didn't give himself up, Má was not going to get out. Marcos got all sad, but I told him off, telling him it wouldn't achieve anything. The lawyer was going to be asking us for money to get the paperwork moving and at least we knew where Má was, not like some people who just disappeared and were never heard from again.

'Remember those women, the ones from the search parties, when they go up the hillside to look for their disappeared family,' I told them. 'Makes me really sad when I see them come past. The key thing right now is to get some money together, but we can't give up school. Má wouldn't like it—'

'But we've got to do something,' interrupted Fredy.

'In the mornings, I'm gonna keep going to school like I always do. In the afternoons, you'll go. But we need to find some work. Go down to the guy who sells *El Metro*, see if he'll let you help him, or down to the crossroads and ask Rulo if he'll let you wash windscreens or something, I dunno, use your brain. Asking around's not a bad idea. As soon as I get out of school, I'll start looking for work for the afternoons and evenings. And we ought to keep hunting for Miguel. At least we know where he might be now. You'll see, Má'll be back soon. So let's get started. Might as well go to the first address.'

It wasn't far, so we wasted no time getting there. It was a greengrocer near the avenue, Frutas San Juan. When we got there, the fruit was piled up on tables and in crates and the smell of onions, apples, pineapples and melons was overwhelming. The owner sold cheese, peanuts and jelly sweets too. He was seeing to some customers and when he was finished, I went over and introduced myself.

'Nah, I've not seen Miguel for months. He did work here for a while, putting out the fruit and helping customers load their bags into their cars when they bought a lot, particularly at the weekends when we sell a lot of onions and avocados for the grills.'

'It's just, we need to find him.'

We didn't say why.

'Well, if he shows up round here, I'll let him know. How did you say you knew him?'

'Um, well, he's my jefa's boyfriend,' I replied, although I almost choked on the words, but it was better than saying nothing.

The grocer let out a guffaw. 'Never imagined Miguel had a woman.'

Ay, Má, who the hell did you take a chance on? I thought.

'Sir, also, if you need any help, we're after some work,' I added.

The man leaned back in his chair and crossed his arms before scratching his elbows as if he had boils. On his desk was an image of the Virgin of the Oak, a large print next to a small unlit candle, as well as towers of ten-peso coins. A man walked in with some bundles of onions and the grocer said to put them at the back. And without a hint of concern, he took out a huge wad of one-hundred-peso notes from his trousers and counted out three hundred pesos.

The smell of fruit and vegetables was very strong, so too was the smell of some that were possibly rotting underneath the crates. Above us, a fan wafted the stale air. At the back of the room hung several calendars displaying a real mix of pictures, from TV actresses to female saints advertising 1994 or 2001. There were stacks of paper rolls in packs of thirty-six. The man looked at them and asked, 'Can you carry those without dropping any?'

Fredy said yes and stepped forwards. He stood looking at the packets for a few seconds until some devil or other nearby picked up the heaviest and gave it to him. Fredy carried it over to the grocer, who laughed.

'Wisdom comes with age, I guess. I can't give you much, 'bout four hundred a week for your brother and some fruit that's on its way out. And if you get any tips, I get half.'

It wasn't very much, considering what Miguel had earnt in a day as an odd-jobber, but given the situation, it was better than nothing.

'My brother goes to school in the afternoon. Can he come mornings and weekends?'

'Done. I'll see you here tomorrow and we'll see how the week goes.' That's all he said to Fredy. 'And good luck finding Miguel. He's probably in a ditch somewhere drowning in booze.'

We headed back home somewhat excited. It was dark now and when we reached El Rancho, Jeno was there with his crew and the woman who ran the lottery. A lot of the local women were there too, playing along, betting with their beans, stones or bottle tops on the boards, the caller singing out the relevant verse each time a numbered card was pulled out, all hoping to win the bags of groceries as their prize.

My brothers carried on walking while I stopped to talk to Jeno. I told him everything. He'd asked around if anyone knew of anyone in the women's prison and he'd been told about three names, but when they'd asked why he wanted to know, he'd said nothing.

'I'm gonna need a job,' I told him.

'Well, you already know it's two grand every two weeks to help me.'

'Who'd I have to watch for?'

'Y'know, the new ones. If you want, I give you a phone and that's that. There's a number you call when you spot anything strange going down in the colonia: feds, soldiers, strangers.'

I imagined Má shaking her head. My Nokia was the cheapest phone there was, and I never had any credit. It was so old it didn't even have any games. Jeno's compas stood a way off, but they were watching us. They didn't like me. They took the piss because I preferred to go to school than hang out on the streets. I didn't think myself any better than them, it just didn't sit well with me, but it was easy money.

I was tempted, about to say yes, but I pulled back. I couldn't live like that, with fear hanging over me, the dread of pick-up trucks and persecutions, of being forced to kill just to survive.

Jeno spat. 'Stop resisting, bro. It's time.'

'Nah.'

'Why you being like this?'

'I dunno, but I am. If I get desperate, I'll come find you, but I wanna see if I can sort it somewhere else first.'

'It's there if you want it,' he replied, disappointed, and he went back to his compas.

It was then, just as I was making my way back home, when the Boss's call came through. Hearing his serious voice didn't give me much hope; after all, it was already dark and I didn't think he worked Saturdays.

'Efraín Martínez?' My palms were sweaty, it felt like they'd turned to water when Raúl said, 'Bad luck, kiddo, they've already moved your jefa to Santa Cecilia, the women's prison. The good news is you can see her on Sundays, well, not this one coming, but in a couple of months, when they let her have visitors.'

'Why so long?'

'That's what the law says, chamaco, I can't tell you why.'

My mind went blank. Everything around me slowly disappeared, like salt when you put it in a pan of water. At first you look at it and it's white, you see its trail in the water as it falls into the liquid, and then it disappears. I wanted to throw up because I suddenly felt like I had a handful of salt on my tongue, burning my teeth and my eyes, the

93

salt forcing me to close my eyelids until at the very back of this saltiness, I heard something sweet: a song. It was a slowed-down colombiana that Má liked, a song about a canoe travelling the waterways of Cesar state, Colombia, leaving the old port for the beaches of love in Chimichagua. The lyrics were accompanied by the heartfelt sounds of an accordion or a violin. So great was my sadness in that moment, I could hear the canoe's oars splashing around me.

That brought me back to reality and to Raúl's final words, 'I'm going to need those extra four thousand pesos I mentioned to you.'

10

The next day I visited the second, third and fourth businesses on the list Miguel's mamá had given to us, with no success. I was already exhausted by the time I decided to try my luck in the last place the guy who had wanted to be my stepfather had worked. It was a store selling damaged goods at a discount over on Miguel Alemán Avenue.

It was a long way from home and I'd had to take two buses which dropped me outside the huge warehouse. Guarding the entrance to the car park stood a concrete Aztec god holding an obsidian sword like the pictures I'd seen in the books at school. An immense crane with massive caterpillar tracks, as big as three trailers put together, took up most of the spaces in the car park. The driver's cabin was squashed, as if it had been smashed with one of those steel wrecking balls. It was a very sunny day.

I went inside and was welcomed by a hellish heat that floated leisurely along the aisles displaying their wares, and some kind of entrance area filled with filthy electric devices. Everything was covered with a layer of dust. A woman watched over the entrance and the cash desks stood nearby, with products piled up on racks. It didn't look like anyone had run a mop around there for years.

I walked along slowly, trying to take it all in. The light filtered in through the asbestos roof. In some places, there was more shadow, in some places more light. On the walls of exposed, unplastered brick hung various posters announcing *Exit, Sale, 2 for 1*. The furniture beyond the entrance area was all damaged. I walked along the first aisle with its offerings of cupboards, wardrobes and cabinets that all looked good at first – so good in fact that you wanted to take a better look – but a closer inspection revealed their defects: one side more faded than the other, one corner bashed in from some impact or other, a hinge that didn't work, a door that had dropped slightly. A few metres further on, the furniture really started to deteriorate and the cemetery began – cupboards, dressers, sideboards, chairs, benches, headboards, all sorts of beds, worn and tarnished, without legs, without some surfaces, some of the wood swollen as if previous water exposure had worn away its shine, TV stands from decades gone by – until all that remained at the end was a pile of random unidentifiable bits and pieces. In the same way, other aisles offered clothing, shoes, kitchen utensils, stationery, unlabelled cans and bags of sweets, all jumbled up, a little bit of everything.

When I finally returned to the entrance, I introduced myself to the woman and asked if she knew Miguel. The name didn't ring any bells for her so she sent me over to Evaristo who might know; he was in there somewhere sorting some things out. I found him with a supermarket trolley full of cans. He looked at me with disinterest when I asked if he was the right person.

'What can I do for you?' he said eventually.

He must have been around thirty-five and while he looked young, his hair was already starting to turn grey. He was very thin, he wore glasses and his shirt was tucked in. If someone wears their shirt tucked in, it means they're someone to look up to, they mean business. I got such good vibes from him that I put my hand out to dap him up like we do back home, and he returned the handshake. Evaristo probably came from the districts too, although, thinking about it, who in this city didn't? The only ones who didn't were a handful of people who lived out southwest, near Chipinque. The whole city was districts and gangs, kids like me who studied and worked hard or those who messed about, taking it easy at school, hanging out down the arcades, or getting high on glue, or playing football at the weekends, tucking into tostadas and fizzy drinks afterwards; normal guys and girls who came out of the factories – Kemet or Focos or Celeco or Denso – wearing their uniforms like they'd just been at a different school, but who looked like they were having a good time with canteens, football pitches or basketball courts. Some of them had wanted to work in candy factories or for Coca Cola or the places where they made ham, but they'd thought better of it because they'd get fat. Ultimately, we were all from the districts.

'I'm looking for an old guy called Miguel Saldívar.'

Evaristo was wiping the cans with a cloth and stacking them on the shelves. 'Yeah, I remember him, but he doesn't work here any more. Left about six months ago. He worked here for a while but between you and me, he was a lazy so-and-so and one evening there was a robbery on his shift, so we fired him. You family?'

'No, God no.'

Even though it was an ugly place, I felt comfortable there. 'It's just he recommended this place as somewhere to get work. Did he stack shelves like you, sir?'

Evaristo laughed. 'No, he was a watchman.'

'I could do that too.'

'That's a big job, chamaco. Not for the likes of you.'

'C'mon, give me a chance. I go to school in the morning, but I can come straight here when I finish.'

The man continued his work.

'Um, how d'you know what everything is?' I pointed to the aluminium cans. Some had dents in the side, others in the bottom.

'I don't. They bring them in like that.'

This was the place where the city abandoned everything: clothes, socks, kitchen utensils, stationery, notebooks, dirty mattresses, shelved furniture, broken television sets. Everything worked but there was always something wrong. But the surprising thing was the store's success. There were quite a few people shopping because everything was so much cheaper.

'You see, sir, I need the work,' I told him eventually, even though it was miles from home, 'and I need it to be here in case Miguel comes back.'

Evaristo shook his head and told me to leave my details with Señora Estela, the lady at the front. If something came up, they'd call me.

'Can you work evenings? All weekend?'

'That's when I'm most free,' I answered.

He looked me up and down again. 'And where did you say you live?'

I had to lie. 'La Talaverna.'

'Ah, close by then. Well, go and talk to Estela and leave your number. And here you go. Tell her I gave it to you.'

He handed me a can from the trolley. It looked like peaches in syrup, then again, perhaps it was pickled chillies. On the way to the checkout, I sniffed it to see if the scent of the contents could somehow escape from its dark, liquid interior, but it didn't. I left my details with Estela who turned out to be very young. When I left it was already late and I rushed into town to hand over the rest of the money to the lawyer.

When I arrived at the office, there was no sign of Estrella. I thought of Irma, how we used to chat at the flea market and then how we talked outside her house, laughing and joking. Her hands were smooth. The thing I liked best about her was her long hair and her eyes – she had a gentle way of looking at you and her eyes always shone like stars. We made out, hot, on the porch of her house, or in the back rooms at school but that's as far as it went.

Where we lived, when you got together, it wasn't long before the babies started to arrive. If she hadn't changed neighbourhood, we'd probably still be seeing each other. Or maybe not, who knows? I had no idea why I thought Estrella could be my girlfriend when I had so many other problems going on. I was losing faith all on my own but seeing her would give me a boost.

Like last time, Señora Maribel gave me a piece of paper stating how much I was giving her, and before I left, she handed me another card.

'This is so you can go to the prison,' she said. 'Get your mamá some clothes – that's what she'll need most inside – some money and some food. Go there, they'll show you into a room and you'll fill out some forms. The staff will pass everything on to her.'

'And when can I see her?' I asked, discouraged as I read all the requirements – birth certificates, addresses, registration numbers, papers I didn't have and didn't know how to get.

'As she's already been processed … it's been a few days, let me see … two weeks already! Well, probably still a while to come. Stay calm, though. Señor Morcillo is seeing her today. He'll probably bring you better news, but you need to understand that this will take some time. Whatever happens, he's introduced himself and given her his number. As soon as he can, he'll fill you in.'

I felt gloomy. I didn't have any food to take to Má, although I could manage some clothes, something useful at least. Who knew what they were giving her to eat in prison, but it wouldn't be anything tasty like she'd usually have. She really knew how to cook.

On my way back home I saw Jeno with his usual gang underneath the Anacahuita. We greeted each other from a distance. I climbed the hill and went inside our house. I felt strong but at the same time, I felt a hole inside me, like garbage buried deep within me, not even food waste, just plastic and nappies (there's nothing more revolting than dirty nappies). I carried all that waste inside me, it accompanied me everywhere. There was no way I could go to school like that the next day. But then I remembered the words of Miguel's mamá, and I imagined them all down there, just a few streets away, sat in their rocking chairs, listening to the old norteñas.

Marcos was already home – they'd let him out early – and I started to warm up some noodles. They weren't as good as Má's but it was something at least. Around eight, Fredy arrived. His shirt was ripped and his nose was bleeding. He splashed water in his face and went and sat angrily on the flat rock outside.

'Who hit you?'

'No one. Leave me alone.'

He said nothing more and threw himself on the bed where Má and Miguel used to sleep. He didn't even take off his shoes, even though I told him to. Eventually, we curled up next to him, but I soon got up again and went to sleep on the foam mat as always because I didn't deserve the comfort, nobody did.

I saw the can Evaristo had given to me that afternoon. I picked it up and held it in my hands. I shook it. It sounded hollow inside. There was something in there, but I couldn't tell if it was sweet or savoury. At midnight I got up and climbed the hill to the place where we hid the money, and I buried the can. I didn't want to get home one day and find that Fredy or Marcos had opened it. The following Sunday, I'd go to the Santa Cecilia prison and take Má some clothes and money, just as the woman had said. I looked at the can in the hole. It barely weighed anything, as if all it contained was air. It seemed light, as if it had found its place on the hillside.

We're all cans without labels. No one knows what the future holds, I thought. *Just like this can of who knows what.* I decided I'd save it. I wouldn't open it until Má was home. I liked the idea that it was full of clouds or songs about canoes; who said it could only contain things steeped in brine or syrup?

11

That night there was a shooting in the colonia below. The clattering of the machine guns cut through the air. Fredy was the first to step outside and look down towards the streets doused in a mercurial light. Once the sounds of gunshot faded away, you could hear the dogs barking.

'Where was it?' I asked him.

'Over there, I think,' he said. He pointed along a path leading to a gated neighbourhood, El Maurel, the only one nearby that was protected by high walls. Inside there was one of those grand villas set in acres of land, and everything. Some of the houses even had three floors. Sometimes we'd spy on them through the binoculars with Jeno, more so since we once spotted a girl in a bikini sunbathing on a terrace.

After the shooting, like five minutes later, a pick-up truck shot out and we heard it brake hard as it reached the avenue. My belly was grumbling from the acid of the grapefruit we'd had for dinner, the day's payment from the greengrocer. I hadn't managed a wink of sleep because I was carrying so much worry, my back felt tense and knotted. It came again, the rat-a-tat-a-tat-a of the machine guns and the deafening bangs of the AR-15 on the other side of the neighbourhood.

'It's all kicking off,' said Fredy. 'I really miss Don Neto. Everything was so much calmer when he was here. It's all such a mess right now cos Jeno isn't strong enough to keep everyone happy.'

Jeno? He thought Jeno was the answer to everything. All we were missing was for the hillside to fill up with Zetas. When I was eleven, up here in El Peñón we knew the gang hid their stuff in the caves further up on the Cerro de la Silla, the hill nearby. They'd ride around the area, going up as far as they could on their quad bikes and then climbing the rest on foot. Sometimes someone higher up would be cooking and the smell of grilled meat would waft down to us and we knew it was them. It wasn't like they were strangers either; they were compas from here and there, older brothers of schoolmates or neighbours.

But then the Golfo gang arrived and ran the Zetas out of town, although I've heard people say they're gathering themselves together again in some parts of the city.

One night, a group of armed men went up there, marching along the narrow paths. They passed the house and continued on up to who knows where. When they came back down, they were carrying goods and whatever else they had found. Má ordered us to stay inside, so we didn't even see the men when they came back down.

'It's the Bogeyman,' she told Marcos, who was younger, but not so young to fully believe her.

It was around that time that Don Neto and his power went up in smoke. Some people say they never caught him. Some say he's still wandering around Juárez colonia, that he occasionally does a tour of the colonia in a black Ford Lobo, but not like before. They also say he's going to come back soon, but others say he was killed that night when those men scoured every inch from El Rancho all the way down to Eloy Cavazos.

The next morning, everything was quiet. Nobody remembered the shooting, or nobody mentioned it at least. A couple of cockerels crowed on my way to school, some pigs were fighting in a pen on the edge of the hillside, women emptied out water onto the pavements and a group of older men sat eating at a taco stand. School was the same as always. It was one of those days where you sit there for five hours, but as soon as the bell rings, you stand up, and – pffff – you've forgotten everything. The girls were talking about some concert they were going straight from school to queue up for, even though they wouldn't get in. The boys were going on about a Rayados match. Now the stadium had moved so close by, they were planning to head down for the match.

I felt cut off from it all, miles away, like I was living a different life and the problems and questions on the board at the front couldn't give me the answers. Like some boring old fart. Like an adult. I was fifteen. I wasn't interested in the parties, or meeting up to work on a group project, or in who was dating who, or wondering whether the teacher Lupita had had dengue fever. By this age, other kids had already dropped out of school. They were already working. They already had kids. They'd be off into the colonias with their jefas. Life.

When class finished, I found Jeno outside. He was always hanging around, selling. He had a new pair of kicks and guitar, they looked good. He was leaning on an old car. We bumped fists. Jeno lit a cigarette and offered me one, but I didn't even know how to smoke.

'What d'you think of my ride? Sick, eh?!'

'It yours?'

'Yep. I did a couple of jobs. Saw it and bought it right there and then.'

The car was an ancient Grand Marquis, the sort the Mafiosos used to drive in the Mario Almada films on TV.

'Hey, d'you know there was a shooting last night?'

'The Zozayas are trying to get in. They're after us.'

'Guess they didn't get you.'

'Nah, we fought 'em off. S'why I got the wheels, so we can get round quicker. They all want those big shiny pick-ups, but no one's gonna suspect an old Grand Marquis like this. I learned that from Don Neto: a low profile keeps you alive longer than the truck of the year. I'm gonna be around, just in case.'

A group of kids approached us and bought a couple of bags. One said hi to me and I said hi back.

'How's all the stuff with your jefa?' Jeno asked.

'Same as before. She's in the Santa Cecilia now.'

Jeno pulled a face. 'Some of our girls are in there. Just say the word, yeah?'

'Nah, bro, I can do it on my own. If it all goes wrong, I'll let you know.'

'By the way, compa, the one person that did approach me was your man, Fredy. Says you need dough and, well, I need someone else, 'specially after last night.'

My blood drained to my feet. 'No way. Fredy?'

'No cap … and seeing as no one knows him, I can help him out. It's just standing there and watching. He's working down the grocer's, isn't he? Great place for him to keep tabs on people coming and going.'

'Aw, nah Jeno, don't do that.'

'Just letting you know.'

I left him selling and on my way back home, I passed Fredy at the frutería, about to head off to school. He'd left home early taking his rucksack with him, his uniform inside. He changed at the grocer's. He was stubborn, and if you told him not to do something, he'd do it anyway, just to piss you off. I said hi just as he was helping a man with a sack of oranges.

I hadn't realised how grown-up he'd been getting; even though he was only in his first year at high school, he wasn't one of those baby-faced kids any more. Fredy was fairly muscly, quite tall, slender, with an adult look on his face much older than his years that revealed the attitude he had inside. His features were beginning to sharpen and his haircut, half shaved like so many others round here, made him someone to watch out for. He got together with some of the other kids and played football at El Rancho, but who knew what they were getting involved with down there.

I looked down at my hands. I ought to be bringing in money. Má's savings had nearly all gone but I needed more cash. I'd been asking for work everywhere. At the petrol station they told me I was too young and they could be fined for hiring me. I'd been down to the traffic lights on the crossroads and tried to find someone who'd share a corner with me to wash windscreens, but I couldn't. I remembered last summer when I'd helped out at Riri's taco stand, so I started doing the rounds of all the taco stands, but no one wanted me for evening work either. As soon as I left school, I started walking and asking for work, in hardware stores, mechanics' workshops, but nowhere was hiring part time – they only wanted someone full time and I couldn't leave school. Bored and miserable, I sat outside the house watching the sunset. I was that close to asking Jeno for help, but I still held back.

One afternoon, my phone rang. It wasn't the Boss, but Estela from the damaged furniture store.

'Efraín Martínez?' she asked.

The next afternoon I went straight there after school. I gave Fredy my rucksack to take home for me. It took two buses to get there. I crossed the car park and soon found Evaristo. He explained briefly that he needed a gofer. My job consisted in stacking shelves, cleaning, helping customers and running errands. Formally, I wasn't employed, but he'd give me three hundred pesos a day to work from two 'til nine, more or less what Má used to earn from her cleaning.

I never carried as much as I carried that day. I sweated like an absolute pig, as they say. There were still a few weeks 'til I'd see Má and my days now felt short between school and the damaged goods warehouse, like I suddenly had no space to do, say, think or play anything else. Every day rolled into the same routine. Get up, go to the bathroom, splash water in my face, chew something, run to school, do tests, say my name during the register, doodle to kill my boredom, copy out notes, laugh at a joke, hunch down so the teacher never picked on me, go to the front, think about Estrella, speak to the Boss, say hi to Jeno, always take things over for Má, always, but never hear any more from her other than she was well.

I'd get home around ten and then start my homework. We saved the food we bought, adding it to the fruit the greengrocer gave us, alternating that with hours of enforced fasting. Má had taught us to boil eggs, heat up beans, but that was all. She'd been a proper cook, and we missed her food.

The damaged goods store took a delivery once a week. Insurance trucks would arrive, or lorries from the big supermarkets and we had to unload whatever we could: boxes of typewriter paper, notebooks, cuddly toys, furniture, stoves without burners, fridges. Sometimes bundle after bundle of clothes would arrive from the USA, baby booties still with their prices in dollars that we had to change to pesos.

The first weekend I worked there, there was no space in the car park, and we had someone out there directing traffic. The things people mostly seemed to be after were electro-domestic appliances with up to seventy per cent off because of a scratch or scrape. The other days, except for Mondays when we were closed, I'd be cutting it fine to arrive by two, and then I'd stay there until nine at night.

One such afternoon, while I was carrying a desk (a survivor from a fire) along a corridor where I was to leave it, my phone rang.

It was Má.

'Mijo! Son!'

I didn't know what to say at first. My palms started to sweat. The phone seemed to have a life of its own and was trying to escape. How could that even happen?

'Mijo, Efraín, it's me.'

I didn't recognise her voice, or perhaps I didn't want to. I looked around me. Everyone was doing their usual stuff. Má's hoarse voice awoke a stream of tears within me that I didn't want to let go. I smiled. I know I smiled so much the happiness flooded into the desk that was missing a leg.

'Oh, come *on*!' she said eventually, and that phrase, the one Má would say to us to get us to hurry up, sent a flood of relief through my body and made me chuckle.

'But—'

'Don't you go messing around, mijo. The other day, a woman came and told me she'd look out for me, that all I need to do is stay out of trouble and keep my head down, so that's what I'm doing. Today, one of the others lent me her phone. And they've given me the clothes you send through the prison staff. Thank you, I like those blouses. At least I can dress how I want in here. How are your brothers?'

Má's voice sounded serious, composed, hard, if you can call it that. I quickly told her what we'd been up to since she'd been in jail. She listened on the other end in silence, without interrupting, and eventually said, 'Don't worry, I'm sorting it all out. Your lawyer came to see me, mijo. Don't be doing anything crazy, those lawyers cost a fortune and I don't want you doing anything stupid.'

I told her we weren't, and that we were still going to school which helped calm her down. Suddenly the call cut off. The silence of the broken call set me on edge, but I couldn't do anything about it. I put my phone away and went back to work. I wanted to tell my brothers asap about what had happened. I rushed through the rest of the afternoon, stacking everything so I could leave and go home as soon as possible.

Evaristo had told me to sort out the section with desks and tables, the dirtiest area of all, right at the back of the shop. I headed down there. I didn't want to miss any calls from Má just in case she managed to call again, so I borrowed some headphones, put them over my ears and connected them to my phone. I put on some music and started working. I was concentrating like never before, as if Má's call had given me an energy I'd lost.

The afternoon started to darken, but I didn't even notice when the gloom crept in around me. Nor did I hear the crash of the light switch as they turned it off. It was summer so there was still a little sunlight, and part of the warehouse was still lit up. I felt full of energy and excitement. I cleaned, I sorted, I stacked the furniture back up again, all submerged in hope. When I finally noticed the shadows, my heart leaped into my mouth. I took off the headphones and moved towards the shop entrance, but it was closed. I banged on the steel shutter. Nothing. I shouted Evaristo's name a couple of times, but no one came.

The watchman. The watchman won't be long and then I can go, I told myself. I tried to calm down, but I wanted to scream with anxiety. When I was little, I used to dream of being locked in the Soriana supermarket near where we lived. I imagined running along the aisles and eating sweets and bread, opening the boxes of Transformers and Playmobil, the best toys I'd never had. I'd eat roast chicken, the ones they have on the rotating spit all day long. I'd eat key lime pie, yogurts, crisps. I could watch TV 'til I fell asleep, stretching out on one of the mattresses in the store. It had been one of my most regular dreams.

If by day and in the light the warehouse felt a little spooky – as if it were haunted by the worn-out crap it had taken in from the world – in the gloom, the place was like a house of horrors. How different from the Soriana of my dreams. The clothes displayed on tall rails looked like rows of people hanging from the gallows. The aisles of cans, electro-domestic appliances, gardening stuff and other equipment turned into grey fortresses where it wasn't hard to imagine nocturnal beasts lurking, goblins with knives and forks, ready to chase after me, their crude chests made of electric toasters, and their infernal eyes brought to life by the on-switches of liquidisers and dressed in yellowing clothing from the sales section.

Of all the animals in the world, the ones I was most scared of were frogs. This was ever since I had once taken a bucket shower in the dark. I'd picked up a scrubber, lathered it with soap and started to wash with it. I'd felt the scrubber slipping in my hand so I'd squeezed it so as not to drop it. It was then that I realised I'd picked up a frog instead of the scrubber and that, soap and all, I'd been rubbing it all around my neck, my chest and between my legs. I screamed, and ever since frogs have been my worst enemies.

I now imagined an army of frogs gathering among the cans. The cans would start to shake nervously, something beating from within. They would fall from the racks, exploding on impact, but instead of peaches in syrup or tuna a la mexicana, frogs of all shapes and sizes would jump out at me, with their fat inflated throats, dead eyes and rough tongues. The frogs would come for me, they'd climb into my mouth, lay their eggs in my intestines and settle down in my lungs with their slimy skin full of poison and pustules. The horror of it all made me want to throw up.

And then, on top of all that, I noticed the worst thing: my phone was dead. I tried to find a charger among the boxes of cables, but not one of them was the one I needed. I walked along to the office, but it was locked. Nobody would believe I'd forced the door in a moment of anguish. I kicked the steel shutter again but still nobody came to my rescue. I sat down on the floor. I started to hear noises, the rats at large having fun. We always caught quite a few in the traps. I stood up and decided to stay close to the main entrance. At least some fresh air flowed through there.

At about one in the morning, I felt hungry. I hadn't eaten all day, only a couple of crunchy duritos with cream and salsa at school. I headed towards the cans and stood there looking at them. I shook a couple to try and work out what was inside, until I settled on a medium-sized one. I scraped it against the floor several times and finally managed to pop the lid. I could never have imagined what was inside: a canned hamburger, with everything, complete with yellow cheese. It was soggy but soft, the cold meat stuck to the bread with a smear of what might have been mayonnaise. I took it out as best I could because it was tightly squeezed in the can. The dust from my fingers left dirty fingerprints on the bread. When I finally had a good hold of it, I lifted it to my nose and sniffed it before taking a bite. I'd got lucky. It didn't taste that bad, a mixture of flavours, plastic, salt, vinegar and sort-of meat – I'd eaten worse things!

Slowly, I started to doze off, far from the ghosts, surrounded by rats and next to a shelf-full of canned hamburgers. When Evaristo opened the door the next morning, he was surprised to see me there.

'I've gotta go,' I told him, somewhere between embarrassed and sleepy. 'I left my brothers on their own. I took a burger in a can, I'll pay when I get back.'

'Efraín, wait …'

But I legged it. I went straight to school, but they wouldn't let me in. So I set off for home, but my body was aching because of where I'd slept, and my eyelids kept drooping. When I reached El Rancho, Jeno was there on a bench made of beer and fizzy drinks bottles. He was smoking a cigar while he made short work of a pile of breakfast tacos. I sat down next to him.

'I put a stop on your jefa, Friar.'

'Huh?'

'Got some protection for your old má down at the Santacilia.'

I didn't know what to say, but I felt completely powerless. I wasn't fit for anything, I was useless. What I wanted didn't matter, as everyone else decided for me. And I was tired. I just wanted to drop. The hunger, the annoyance all took over me, and yet I still managed to say, 'I didn't ask you for anything.'

'You didn't, but little Fredy wanted us to help, so it's all good. Relax. He just gonna be watching, yeah, like I told you. No one's gonna say nothing, no one else knows, it's like it never even happened, an agreement between him and me. I won't tell no one higher up. I just had a chat with your man and he's gonna be helping me out. S'all gonna be much calmer for your jefa now. I've given Fredy a walkie-talkie and everything.' Then he held out some notes to me. 'For the lawyer, take it.'

'So what? You Don Neto now?'

Jeno smiled. 'Oh, c'mon, lighten up … Just take it, shut up and eat some tacos.'

He pushed the polystyrene box over to me: two pork belly tacos smothered in green salsa that looked delicious, served up with shredded cabbage and tomato. The taste of the canned hamburger still lingered in my mouth.

'Nah, no way, Jeno, we didn't ask for none of this. I'll tell Fredy to give you back the radio.'

Jeno got all defensive, swore, and pulled the box back, taking a large bite from one of the tacos.

'Yeah, well, whatever. No going back now. But I'll look out for him, so just chill, yeah? We're compas, aren't we?'

He pushed the notes towards me again; we needed them so badly. As I took the money, I felt an ugly, crushing pressure in my chest, like it would tear me in two. I thought of Fredy and Má. Even now I don't know why I did it. Honesty is a prison too. I headed away from El Rancho.

Pinche Fredy, that was it, he was no longer under my control. I'd lost him. He wasn't Má's any more, or mine, but I had to accept it. Chingado. I had to accept it; we needed that money. That day I learned how it felt to swallow my pride. We had to get Má out. This was Fredy's contribution to the cause. Whatever happened next, it would all come back to this moment. I stuffed the money to the bottom of my pocket. I'd give it to the Boss as soon as I could.

12

You have to be careful on the streets. You have to learn to look around. To be suspicious. Every noise. Every movement. Every car that drives up Montes Azules could be dangerous. If there's a stranger wandering around, it's a warning; if someone claims to be 'lost'. Look. Watch. Check. Assess the danger.

In the following days, learning to look around to work out what Fredy was doing was my only tool to find the words to face up to him. His decision had surprised me. Didn't he know where we were? Hadn't he heard the stories? Everything was so much worse now than it was before. I didn't just have to get Má out of prison, I had to keep Fredy safe too.

From high up at our house, from that same spot where I'd followed the police convoy that had come for Má, I now kept watch. The air took on the smell of damp earth, drifting over from the other side of the hill where a fine,

fine rain was falling, the sort where you don't even realise it's raining, but you get soaked anyway. Dark clouds squeezed together over the mountain before the first clouds left the hillside for the city. The weeks since Má had been taken hadn't been easy. The money in the tub had nearly all gone – I'd handed over the last few notes to Raúl – but Fredy was openly bringing in more, now he had nothing to hide. The people from the Human Rights Commission still hadn't replied. All that money thrown down the drain. Money only ever moved from one hand to the other, it never changed anything. It didn't bring freedom. It didn't bring love. It didn't bring peace. Notes only ever came and went.

I looked down towards El Rancho as a pick-up parked up and Jeno and the others got out. I stepped inside and saw Marcos, bored. I hadn't gone to the warehouse that Saturday because it'd had been closed down. (It happened sometimes, Evaristo told me. 'People come, they buy, and then they complain. Nobody ever said that everything in those cans is edible. We'll be back and I'll let you know.') Fredy was going to be a while yet at the greengrocer's.

Marcos looked more like Papá than any of us. He had a long face, his chin jutted out a little and he had small ears, just like Papá. He looked worried. I barely spoke to him, except about the same stuff Má told us to do. Same with Fredy. We didn't really talk much, but I'd started giving him some advice. *If there's a shoot-out, don't play the hero, just run. Always dress in black in case you need to flee into the night.*

Fredy listened to me, incredulous, but he nodded. The relationship between my brothers was better – they talked to each other more – but I was a stranger.

'I'm bored,' said Marcos. 'Can we go into town?'

'Bet, let's go.'

We quickly changed our T-shirts and set off down the footpaths. We always kept our eyes on the ground as we walked because there was usually some water or gas pipe that crossed the path and sent us flying, or a big root from the trees that had just sprung up, or water gushing out from a blocked drain. Some pigs trotted happily passed us heading up the hill, four of them, fat and dirty, sniffing at something or other on the ground. Once down in the colonia, we passed the internet and Xbox café. There was a queue of people waiting to take on the challenges and all you could hear was the music, gunshots and explosions coming from the screens.

A lady selling duritos with salsa, cream and sliced cabbage hurried past with icy beers. Further on, a man was listening to a rebajada, while another was cleaning a grill with an onion. Every weekend, the neighbourhood would fill with smoke as almost everyone lit a charcoal fire to grill meat, chicken or sausages. Every porch became an extension of a day out in the countryside. People would come together to chat, drink, listen to music and later on, fight. There was always someone who'd get their fists out, or even a knife, to threaten some distant cousin, father or brother once the beer took them to the accusations stage.

As I had the money from my work at the warehouse, the plan was to head down to the area around Reforma Street to buy some pirated CDs and perhaps stop off for some tacos. We walked quickly, excited because this was the first time in ages that we'd been out.

We reached the frutería. Fredy was lugging bags of charcoal, so we let him know where we were going. He straightened up when he saw me, as if being with Jeno had made him stronger and unleashed something within him. I'd seen it with the other local kids, timid boys who changed once they got in with the narcos, coming out of themselves. Money gave them power, and the knowledge they were carrying weapons gave them a strange sort of courage, like an imposter, false but aggressive at the same time.

A kid is only a kid 'til some narco puts an AK-47 in his hands or starts to give him money to buy things he thinks he needs but doesn't. A kid with a weapon becomes something else, unsure if they're a boy or a man, a victim or a perpetrator, a hitter or a person disappeared. A kid with a weapon who suddenly has it taken away from them at gunpoint ends up running away. They cry as they flee along the footpaths, chased by someone bigger. They're trapped, flushed out and dragged from their hiding places to be taken somewhere they don't want to go, to be scared

121

in ways they didn't even know existed. If they're lucky, they'll be shot and be done with it. If they're lucky, they'll be shot somewhere they're known, by people who can tell their mamá or papá, and they can be buried in one of the municipal graveyards. Here on the rock, on El Peñón, we all know that; it's common knowledge. It causes no alarm, gives no rise to boasting. That's what happens if you're lucky. And if you're unlucky? No one wants to be unlucky.

'Yeah, go,' Fredy said to me. 'I'll just be here. D'you need cash for Marcos?'

'I've got it,' I replied drily.

The bus soon arrived. There were no free seats, so we stood the whole way, right at the back. Close by were a couple of girls about my age, faces fully made up. They chatted about a fiesta they'd been to the night before. Marcos stood behind me. Eventually we reached the crossroads where we needed to get off. We still had to walk the rest, but we were happy to get moving. The streets were packed, people getting off one bus mixed with those getting off another, people stopping to eat sweet gorditas sprinkled with sugar, or to buy elotes topped with sour cream and salsa. Music – norteñas and cumbias – blared out of almost every business. A women's clothes shop had five mannequins in swimsuits with a man out front on a microphone, inviting everyone to buy.

We carried on. We left behind the Colegio Civil university building and then the Juárez market. A cold gust of air blew down the avenue and I turned to look back at the Cerro de la Silla where we lived, now buried among the rain clouds. Marcos wanted something to eat but I told him to wait. Finally, we reached the stalls on Reforma Avenue. Wow, the stalls here! Who hadn't dreamed of blowing all their money there?

The stalls stretched out across five streets between the avenues of Juárez and Cuauhtémoc. In the first block were stalls selling computer games and consoles. We stopped off there first to watch the games. There were always people playing, 'specially the owners who loaded the PlayStations or Nintendos with *Fifa* or *Need for Speed* or *Halo*. Everyone crowded around full of nostalgic memories of playing the games, first on a computer and then on the consoles. There were always loads of people, and some stalls put on challenges or one-day championships. Marcos picked up the games, read the back of the cases and then we watched the screens. We didn't even have a Nintendo or anything, but what wouldn't we have given to have one?! We only just had a large TV that Má had bought two years ago at Coppel and still hadn't finished paying off.

We spent about an hour wandering around this block, until our bellies started rumbling. We crossed through the next block with its stalls selling clothes, belts, shirts and coats, and made a beeline for the third street, the one between Méndez and Jiménez, where we spotted the food outlet we liked. It was the very first stall in the line, near a drain where other stallholders tipped their dirty water. The taco stand had a huge hot plate and their speciality was pulled beef tacos. Mountains of guacamole were on offer in two giant bowls, you could see whole chunks of avocado. We ordered two portions that came super quick and then we smothered the tacos in spoonfuls of guacamole. They passed over two bottles of cola and we found a small corner among all the people. The tacos were delicious, the salsa perfectly cooked and the fizz of the Coca-Cola just ideal.

I had just finished mine and ordered another portion to share when I saw her walk past: Estrella. She was with one of her friends, walking confidently through the last few stalls of women's clothing. I stood up, and almost knocked her over.

'Hi,' I said, feeling like a clumsy oaf.

She seemed surprised to see me there. Her friend even more so. Marcos too.

'Hi …'

'Hi …'

I felt nervous and I immediately asked myself why the hell I was talking to her. It had taken me almost a year to whip up the courage to talk to Irma. I turned back round to face Marcos and I felt surrounded by the aromas of the grill, the fat the meat was cooked in, the sour smell of the onions and the coriander I'd eaten. I scratched my hands in my trouser pockets.

'So, what's new?' I'd never been particularly great at chatting girls up.

Estrella looked at her friend. 'Not a lot, we're just here shopping.'

'Not working with your uncle today?'

That question surprised her and she blushed and took a couple of steps back. 'No, not today.'

'We're just finishing, d'you fancy some tacos?'

She and her friend looked at each other again and smiled. 'No, no thanks …' she answered.

'Shall we go to the shopping mall?' Estrella's friend said to her. She smiled at Estrella and tugged briefly on the sleeve of her blouse. They both smiled nervously, or mockingly, I wasn't sure which.

Just then my brother came over.

'This is my brother,' I said, saying the word *brother* in English.

They didn't say hi. Marcos looked at me questioningly, as if asking what exactly was going on.

'Well, we'll be off, then,' said Estrella.

'If you like, we can come with you. I can show you where to get the best stuff, straight from the States. Some of it's dead cheap … but all completely genui—'

'No, um … no. Thanks,' Estrella interrupted, embarrassed, and then, as if trying to retake control of the situation and insert some distance, she added, 'How's your mamá? Is she out of jail yet?'

I stayed silent. Her friend was visibly shocked and tugged again on her shirt sleeve, letting out a small giggle, definitely nerves this time. And then she looked at us with fear in her eyes, as if we were about to mug them right there and then. I swallowed the bitter taste and answered, 'No, not yet, but your uncle is great. Fingers crossed she'll be out soon.'

'Well, good luck,' she said, and they walked off, not continuing along Reforma with all its stalls but taking a diagonal path to get out of here.

Marcos smiled. 'No way. *She's* your *friend*?' he asked.

I shook my head. Well, no, we weren't anything, just my pure imagination. We carried on wandering through the stalls, no longer that excited, until the stall holders began packing up at the end of the day. Then we made our return journey through the emptying city. We had nowhere to be, so we took our time. And when we got to the bus stop, we had to wait an age. We got off where we always do and started up the hill. Just then a riot police van drove past us, up Montes Azules Road, and I felt the hot gaze of one of the officers on me.

It reminded me of Ramón.

Ramón was a graffiti kid and his bag had always been full of spray cans. The feds picked him up one time and one of them covered his neck in black spray paint. Ramón told me that two of them grabbed his arms and twisted him to the ground, while the other shook the can. Ramón heard the ball-bearing inside knocking and knocking, and then he felt the spray paint all over his neck, dripping. The fumes made him cry, stinging his eyes like they were burning, his skin too, and he felt like puking. But the chota didn't stop spraying the can 'til it was completely empty. Then they let him go. At first, he was walking around all dizzy. Nobody would let him on a bus, so he had to walk for miles to get home, confused from the paint that was dripping down onto his chest.

We'd heard loads of stories like that.

When we got back to El Rancho, it was all saintly quiet. The smell of cooking meat still wafted above the neighbourhood's streets, the last bars of music drawing to a close for the day; the last sounds of gunshots and explosions petered out from the video game store, the last voices of the old women playing the lottery faded, the last remnants of the world ebbed away from our lands; that's how the night slowly died. In El Rancho, there was barely any activity, just people packing up their stalls from the flea market. The sun had melted everything, the hillside, the streets, the houses, life itself.

When I got home, I found Fredy lying on Má's bed with his shoes on. A phone rang, a new one. My brother jumped up in fright. He answered it. His skin turned pale. I saw the fear flood into his eyes. He rushed towards the door, but before he left, he turned and from underneath Má's bed he pulled out a pistol. A short gun. Eight bullets.

'The guys from the Zozaya gang've been seen,' he said.

'Nah, cabrón, stay here, yeah?'

'No way, Friar. If *I* don't go, they'll kill you both.'

'Give it to me then,' I begged.

He was right. He couldn't stay. Someone had to go.

'Stay here,' I ordered.

And I headed out into the darkness.

13

D'you see 'em?

Nah.

That way.

Keep goin', keep goin' … Where are they?

Come on, quick, over there.

Nah, cabrón. Slow down!

Valdo tagged along too, he's right behind.

You drivin' like a psycho.

Keep goin', that way.

That 'em?

Put your foot down!

Eh, cabrón, quit spinning the wheels!

There! There! Got 'em.

Get down, get down … So, cabrones, what's goin' on? Who are you?

Who's asking?

What d'you mean, who's asking? What you doing out here? Don't you know who we are? We la lumbre, cabrón, we in charge round here.

Eh, put it down, yeah? We from round here, Señora Firia's.
I don't know you, bro.

We live here, yeah, eh … Valdo, Valdo, we're Valdo's compas, we went to school down at the Martinez, eh, Valdo, help me out. Ask him, ask him, he's just comin'.

All right, Pirrín, s'up?

S'up, Valdo? They bustin' my ass. What's goin' on? We compas, yeah?

What y'all doing here, messing about this time of night? The Zozayas are on our turf and we thought it was you. How'd it be if we shoot first then ask questions?

Nah, man, we been at the night markets, just left.

Whatever, Pirrín, but let us know it's you, yeah? You nearly got beats for free. What you got there anyways?

S'all above board, just food.

Well, dish it out then, given you scared us like that.

All right, all right. Give 'em some of those leftovers.

What d'you mean leftovers, Pirrín? I don't want no leftovers. You got any tortillas?

Yeah, yeah, help yourselves.

The whole time I was pressed up against the seat, unarmed. Jeno was the first one surprised to see me, but he quickly pushed me into the back seat. I felt a hole in my belly. It was

130

the only way I could think of to save Fredy. *Don't take the easy route*, I told myself. *Just this once.* Further up, the lights of the colonia sparkled on the hillside.

For years, the colonia had been quiet. The feds and la lumbre – the narcos from the cartels, Los Zetas, Los Golfos or La Federación, the ones who used these streets to sell, the ones whose names we avoided saying – everyone had calmed down. Nothing much had happened round here since the Federación guys had moved in and Don Neto had disappeared. They'd been weird years. Since we'd first arrived here, we knew we had to dig in deep, or rather, I didn't know it, but Má had told me, millions of times. Má made it very clear: work, work, work. Whatever it might be, whenever it might be, as long as it was decent, something that would never compromise your future. *What future?* I thought. *What was the point?* You worked and worked, all for three hundred pesos a day, sometimes not even that. How the hell were we ever meant to escape our poverty if we needed luck to even make it to the avenue?

Then there was the other side: join the gangs, sell snow like Jeno, drive a car, buy whatever you like, be free to walk around, but with a healthy dose of paranoia to teach you how to defend yourself from everyone else, more danger involved. Putting your life in God's hands.

I'd known Jeno since we were little kids and he'd always been like that, facing up to the world, daring. He wasn't scared of anything. Now I realised he had become one of

131

the leaders of the neighbourhood narcos. Maybe he'd never been down at the bottom of the ladder as I'd always thought, maybe he'd always been further up. In his first week at high school, he'd ended up in a fight with two other kids, the teachers too. They almost expelled him, but he managed to hang in there until things got really ugly in the colonia and he shipped out.

It was around that time they killed Luisfe down on the avenue. I heard about it and went running down the hill with Jeno. We were both younger then and moved much quicker. Luisfe had been our compa since we'd first met in the fourth year at primary. He was the best goalkeeper in the colonia – even the big kids wanted him on their side. When we got there, there were heaps of patrol cars and Marine pick-ups. Our friend was lying there on the ground, covered by a blanket.

'He knew they were after him,' Jeno told me as the TV cameras trained in on our friend, 'but he didn't want to leave.'

On the way back, he told me they were after him too. 'I didn't do nothin', well, nothin' serious … but Don Neto's told me to go and I'm gonna listen to him.'

He went for a year, the worst year of all, leaving school halfway through, and scarpered. A year later he came back to school because his job now was to pass goods between the pupils and other people who did their buying outside. Jeno lived with his grandmother, his abuelita. The lady didn't seem to worry about it or perhaps she simply never said anything, we never knew which.

'Efra,' he told me once, 'the teachers don't care about us. They come here to get paid, s'all. And if you keep on at 'em, one day they won't even bother.'

We'd barely started school and he already knew: people can be worn down and for him, nothing was easier. Wear them out so they give up, stop fighting and then people like him come along and take everything. Or they snatch it.

And there we were now, in the car, following the Zozayas or whoever it was trying to worm their way in. 'Those kids are put out quicker than a candle,' Má had told me one afternoon, when she discovered I was hanging out with Jeno. And just like that, almost as she spoke, things got really ugly in the colonia and people around here started dropping like flies.

One Friday there was a shooting down at El Rancho, just as everyone had gathered together. They killed like four, but nothing ever appeared in the newspapers. Then they smoked Vicente and Jorge down on the avenue while they were eating tacos. Nothing ever appeared about them either. The go-between to the newspapers didn't even share the news. We heard the nocturnal shots from where we were at home, our ears and eyes glued to the windows. Once, a stray bullet even fell on the house, I heard it clear as a whistle as it plopped onto the metal roof. That was before Má had saved enough for the concrete one. The bullet didn't pierce it though. Pum, pum, rat-a-tat-a-tat-a, pum, silence, then another rat-a-tat-a-tat. Car ambushes, persecutions. You could hear everything up there. Sometimes I did go out at night because really, nobody down there was going to see me all the way up here. You could watch the chase happening in the colonia down below. It was really weird watching them, like watching a film, only that this one could get you killed.

During those years, loads of the compas we played football with disappeared. I don't know if it's true, but they say they're buried up here on the hillside, further up, in the caves where nobody goes, where they used to store the goods. That's where the graves that aren't really graves are, barely even mounds of stones, just piled one on top of the other, stones and dust.

I don't know if there are ghosts on the hillside, but sometimes I hear sounds – a wailing coming from the ravines – and a cold air blows in from elsewhere and falls onto the neighbourhood. When this happens, everyone gets snappy and we all hate each other a little bit more. Being here, resisting here, it weighs on us more heavily. This place where we have to fight for every damn thing, like carrying water or gas canisters up the hillside. I even get the feeling that the vegetables grow more slowly in the small plots where some of the neighbours plant tomatoes, chillies and potatoes, and the pigs that roam as they please seem so bored they want to throw themselves off the hillside. I feel like I want to quit school, get out of there and start working like everyone else, but then I remember the other future that Má wants for us, for Fredy, Marcos and for me.

And I remember, we're good people. That's all she wants from us, work hard and stay out of trouble.

I'm fine with that because I like studying, but I'm not particularly smart. It's clear Fredy likes numbers and Marcos is still too young to know. I'll probably have to give up school soon anyway and start working so we can get Fredy into the preparatoria and he can keep studying after he turns fifteen. Can you imagine how that must feel? Going to the prepa, wearing whatever you like, no uniform! And studying, being *that* person.

Huddled down in the back seat, hunting the Zozayas, I couldn't stop thinking about Estrella. She'll probably go on to some posh prepa or other; her lawyer uncle'll help pay the fees. Why the hell would she even look at someone like me, small fry, who might not even finish high school, and whose má is in jail accused of nicking a mattress?

I spat, something I rarely do, but I needed to get rid of that sour taste in mouth. It was all over. Jeno was pleased I was there, I could tell. I suddenly realised that if Valdo hadn't known Pirrín, they'd have killed him on the spot.

I swallowed.

Eventually, they handed over the food pots, we climbed into Jeno's Grand Marquis and headed back up to El Rancho. When we got there, I found Fredy by the Anacahuita. He looked worried, desperation darting about his eyes. He came over and helped the others with the food, something so he could feel useful. He glanced at me, angry. The boys fetched a couple of beers and started drinking. A couple of others brought out some cigarettes, and someone else took the pots they'd given us. They perched the pots on some rocks and started to help themselves. They'd take a tortilla, lay it across their hand, and using it like a beak, they'd dip it into the stew, grab hold of the meat, and bring out the now-filled tortilla, quickly stuffing it into their mouths. They chewed appreciatively, pleased with their loot.

'False alarm, then,' said Jeno turning to me. 'Good you came.'

'Yeah.'

'So, what now?' He looked pleased.

'Now nothin', just didn't want Fredy to go. He's still young.'

Jeno smiled. The rest of the gang kept eating, my brother helping them. I turned to look at my compa, Jeno. I got up close and, as seriously as I could, I said, 'This isn't the life for my brother, Jeno. Let him go.'

'Where to?'

'Home, yeah? Like before.'

'Naw, cabrón … we helpin' your old jefa an' all.'

'Fine, I'll pay if that's what you want, but then, just let it go.'

'Nah, no way. An' it was me that first took you to that lawyer.'

'Yeah, I know. But let him go. I'm grateful, but it'll just get worse when Má gets out, you know how it is. But now …'

'Now, what?'

'What would've happened if that was the Zozayas?'

'We'd've filled 'em with lead, that's what.'

Fredy looked pale. He said nothing, but he clenched his jaw, giving me the side-eye while we were talking.

'If Fredy's out, he can tell me himself,' demanded Jeno, angry now.

We both turned to Fredy. The rest of the boys kept eating, watching us out the corner of their eyes. I felt the tension in the air. The laughter had disappeared; all you could hear was chewing, the mouths, the teeth.

'I'm here,' Fredy replied, coming over, a taco in his hand. 'And if somethin' needs to be said to Má, it'll be me that says it. I'm the one who asked Jeno for work, so I'll be the one who does it. By the way, Efraín, you forgot this.' He presented me with the pistol.

'Pinche Friar!' my friend swore, laughing. 'You bottled it! You put us at a disadvantage.' Then, turning to my brother, he added, 'That's that then. No biggie, eh, Pinche Friar? Dunno why you gettin' involved here. I know you one of them swots, but not everyone's cut out for school an' that. We'll take care of Fredy. It's cool you wanna protect him – I respect that – but the kid spoke and now he gotta stand by it.'

I thought about the tombs up on the hillside again. Jeno had said the last bit in a spikier voice, each word emphasising just how serious he was.

I'd lost.

One of Jeno's crew walked over to the Grand Marquis and turned on the radio.

'C'mon, Fredy. Let's go eat with Marcos,' I insisted.

My brother turned his face towards the others. 'No. I'm staying here with the compas.'

In that moment something broke. I saw it, everyone's smiles, how they looked at each other, Jeno's defiant expression, something that seemed to announce the storms that would follow. How long would these kids last in the narco world? One, two, three years for the most switched on? They'd all end up dead or in jail. The ones who kept mostly out of it might scarper, but they'd be the minority. Fredy walked over to his new clique and, like them, he put his hand out for a beer. He opened it in front of me and took a few gulps. He didn't like the taste. I thought of Má, how she'd cook us chorizo salsa and bring the freshly made tortillas to the table, still slightly puffed up. They'd deflate before reaching us and we'd quickly fill them with beans and salsa and bring them to our mouths.

I spun 180 degrees and left, walking over the bridge between El Rancho and the colonia. I took a new route along the footpaths, and when I arrived home, I realised I'd felt this peace before.

It was the calm before the storm.

14

We had an appointment to see the lawyer the following Monday afternoon. Fredy and Marcos didn't go to school and came with me into the city instead. We didn't speak on the way, each one of us looking elsewhere, avoiding each other's gaze. The driver of the 209 bus was listening to an old colombiana Má sometimes listened to on a Saturday afternoon, when she got back from cleaning houses. She'd sit there on the big square rock, take off her sandals and dunk her feet in a bucket of water. Then she'd pull out a cigarette from somewhere or other and smoke it slowly, while the hillside breeze gently ruffled her hair and the hem of her skirt. She only ever smoked the one, that was her mantra: one a week, and even then, not always.

Má liked those old songs, the ones about the guadales – the Argentinian quagmires – that weep because they too have a soul, songs about home sweet home, glorious Colombia which sang with sounds of guacharaca birds, the accordion and guitar. She'd buy a few cassette tapes down at the market, not that many people sold them, just one old man who also sold Beta videos in dirty packaging. Má used to play the cassettes and with the music playing in the background, she'd sew clothes or mop the floor, using the time to clean our house or tend to our little garden behind.

We reached the city, got off where we always do and started walking. I hardly had any money left, and the job at the warehouse didn't pay as much as I'd thought. I was going to have to resign and find something else. Fredy kept giving us money, but that went quickly too.

When we got to the lawyer's building, there was nobody in the lobby and my brothers were scared to go in. They'd never been there before, and while the building wasn't anything particularly special, it was still imposing. We went up in the lift and arrived at the top floor. We walked down that same corridor. It smelled of perfume, but I wasn't sure where the scent was coming from. Inside, it felt stifling. I knocked on the office door and Estrella opened the door. I almost turned around and walked away again when I saw her. She smiled like we'd never met before.

'Go on in, my uncle's waiting for you.'

We did as she told us, but my brothers stayed in the waiting room while I went through on my own. Inside, the Boss was looking through some files. The office had no window and a low ceiling; I felt like I was in a mouse cage. I really needed to look for another job. I'd spent days thinking about trying to find something else.

'How have you been, Efraín?'

'Yeah, good, Boss. Just plodding along as always.'

'Good, good, that's what we want to hear. Are you still sending things to your mamá through the prison staff?'

'Yes, Boss.'

'Well.' The lawyer scratched his head. 'Did you know your mamá got beaten up?'

The words were barely out of his mouth when I felt my blood freeze. She hadn't called me again. I wished Fredy was there to hear how his compas were getting on.

'Inside, there are three choices, Efraín: either work for the other prisoners, join a Christian group and cosy up to the Padre, or keep yourself to yourself, away from everyone. I think that's what your mamá's been trying to do, and that's why they beat her up. Someone wants her to do their dirty work. They let me see her yesterday. She's not looking good, but your mamá's strong, that much is very clear. Did you find this Miguel fella?'

I shook my head. How the hell were we going to find him? It was like he'd disappeared off the face of the earth, like he'd been picked up by the wind and dropped God knows where.

'Are you going to need more money?' I imagined where this conversation was leading.

'Yes and no, Efraín. Let's stay calm, OK? I've had an idea I'd like to run past you, partly because the Human Rights Commission still hasn't come back to me. And we can use this beating to help us. I'm going to ask them to move her from the prison wing she's on. It'll still be the same prison, but it might be a fresh start for her.'

I crossed my arms.

'I also want to ask for a consideration that is a little unconventional – they call it a judgement to uphold her good name. I heard about it from a gringo who's coming here as a consultant lawyer. Do you know what that is? No, OK. Well, it's not particularly complicated, but it has – how to explain? – humanity, that's it, that's the word. It has *humanity* at its core. When a Mexican or a Latino is sent to prison in the USA, sometimes, when their personal situation is complicated, for example, if they're coming from a broken home, or, they're coming from—'

'From fuck all, you mean, like where we're all coming from?'

'I wouldn't put it quite like that, but yeah. They send a lawyer to investigate their circumstances, their family, the people they know, to collect evidence, information they can add to their file, so that if there's a trial, they can seek justice that way. I know it's not something we hear about often in this country, but they call it a judgement to uphold her good name. If your mamá is as good a person as you say she is, if she's kept herself to herself in prison to the point

142

they're beating her up because nobody's protecting her inside, if she actually never stole anything, well, perhaps we can give it a try.'

'So, what do we need?'

'Well, just that, we need your má's good name. Find people who would be prepared to give a testimony of good faith before the judge – her employers, people she knows. That, together with the ridiculous evidence the police have, the abuse she's received in detention and the unusual display of force by the police – I've not forgotten you were beaten up that first time you came here. But what can I say, in this country, they put people away for stealing a can of tuna, for crimes a la Jean Valjean.'

'Valjan'

'Jean Valjean ... you've not come across him?'

'Who's he?'

'A character from a novel ... Anyway, here's the deal: find me at least ten people who will testify on behalf of your mother. And bring more money, your má needs it inside. The waiting time's up and you're allowed to start visiting on Sundays, but it's probably best if you don't go right now, given how she is just at the moment ... that's another reason I wanted to see you today ... Here are the papers you need.'

'But, Boss, is Má OK?'

The words were barely out my mouth, and a weary look came over the lawyer. He took some documents out of his desk along with some photographs. 'I took them the other day, to make it clear that your mother's at risk where she is. They're pretty brutal. You don't have to look if you don't want to.'

But I did.

There she was with her face black and blue, one of her eyebrows had been split (you could see the bruise and the skin where they'd stitched it back together) and they'd bust her lip. Another photograph showed her from behind, purple bruising on her ribs, violet marks running down her back, like hurtful, stabbing blemishes. I pressed my lips together. I cursed Miguel. I cursed the mattress.

The lawyer came over and clapped me on the shoulder. 'It's ugly, isn't it?'

'Messed up, Boss.'

'And I've got some bad news for you.'

'More?'

'Your mamá asked for you not to visit her in jail. In a few days you'll be allowed to go see her, but she won't come out, so don't bother going. She doesn't want you to see her in there, says she doesn't want to leave you with that picture of her, that she'd regret it and that she hopes you understand.'

'But Boss ...'

I suddenly felt really sad. I felt a spider climbing up my throat, biting me just below my mouth. Má. Always looking out for us. She'd prefer to be alone than make us worry.

My eyes must have been watering because the lawyer stood up and said, 'Come on, let's take you somewhere to distract you from all this.'

We stepped out of the office and the lawyer spoke to Estrella who gave us an encouraging smile. The five of us left together. Being in among everyone else in the street, being in a group, gave me a certain feeling of calm. Estrella went first, then Raúl, Marcos and me in the middle, with Fredy at the back.

The Boss told me he'd always wanted to be a lawyer. 'I know we have a bad rep, but that's all down to TV.'

He grew up in the Sada Vidrio district, and his parents had helped him to study so he now helped his nieces and nephews. That's how I discovered one of his nephews worked for him before, but he'd taken the 'wrong path towards engineering', he'd said. 'Better they work for me rather than somewhere random.'

We were walking deeper and deeper into the central neighbourhood until we reached the narrow alleyways of the city centre, near the businesses that make disposable bags, polystyrene trays and plastic forks. Eventually, we found ourselves in a very narrow street – there was only room for one car – not far from the Playa bus stop, near the Del Sol department store on Juan Ignacio Ramón Avenue. We reached a large, two-storey house with a garden in the middle and a garage. A grey dog, one of those really woolly ones, came out to greet us. Estrella played with the dog; she stroked its head, and it lifted itself up onto its hind legs and nearly knocked her over. It was called Brandy. In one of the upstairs windows, I saw an enormous picture of a blue whale. We followed Estrella up an even narrower staircase and popped out on the terrace, the entrance just off to one side. It was a bookshop. On the back wall was another painted whale, but even bigger. Bookshelves, and a beautiful piece of wooden furniture filled with tiny books, completed the scene.

The Boss greeted the girl behind the counter and ordered coffees for us: a *frappuccino* for Estrella, two *lattes* for us, an *espresso* for himself. Fredy didn't want anything. I had no idea there were so many different types of coffee. Má only ever gave us a spoonful of Nescafé in a morning, nothing else. We tiptoed around the edge of the bookshop, not daring to properly go in. Quiet music played from some speakers and in an immense glass chiller were countless cupcakes alongside two delicious-looking chocolate cakes. I felt weird but Estrella browsed the shelves like it was the most normal thing in the world, so I copied her. Marcos didn't move, like he was stunned by all the decoration.

I wondered whether I'd have had the guts to walk in here on my own, and the answer was a definite no. I only ever went to the usual places alone or with the same people. In my head, I could only ever have a certain type of girlfriend, or house, or job, or friends. I let out a sigh of fear, but I tried not to lose control. I was watching a very simple picture: a girl standing at a shelf in a small bookshop on a terrace in the city, and for a moment, I wanted to be a part of it too, so I started to wander between the bookshelves, browsing.

Marcos followed me, but Fredy left, crossing the terrace to wait for us down on the street.

From where we were, you could see the trees down on the Macroplaza, and beyond them, the Cerro de la Silla, but from this distance, you couldn't make out the individual houses, just the clear hillside, dyed a dry green hue because of the long heatwave. Marcos kept glancing at the cakes, so I asked the girl how much a slice would cost. I was surprised it wasn't more expensive, so I bought a slice and a cold drink.

'You can eat it in the other room.'

The Boss was already there, flicking through some magazines. The air conditioning chased away the heat. Eventually, Estrella appeared holding a book and she sat down to read it. 'It's called *Ciudades de papel*,' she said. '*Paper Cities*. I've read the whole series.'

'What's it about?' Marcos asked.

Estrella handed it to him, and although it had a lot of pages, it was very light.

'It's really cool! It's about this girl who gets revenge on her ex-boyfriend, she goes off in a car with his best friend and well, lots of stuff happens.'

'Oh.'

'D'you want some?' I pointed to the cake.

Estrella blushed and shook her head. 'I already ate. Thanks.'

The Boss carried on reading, but he watched us out of the corner of his eye, without joining in the conversation.

Then he looked out the window and must have seen Fredy out there because he said, 'Do you want to take something for your brother?'

'No.'

'Take him something … How's he coping with it all? He's tough, yeah?'

'Something like that, but that's his problem, Boss.'

A flock of parrots had settled in a huge tree in the garden. Marcos passed me the book and I started reading, not a lot, because I felt like they might chase us out of there at any moment, but little by little, the story pulled me away from my worries, even Má, beaten up in jail. About an hour and half later, the Boss gave me some cake for Fredy, and Estrella gave the book to Marcos, buying another book by the same author for herself. We said goodbye in the street and they headed off north.

Must be sick to have an uncle or aunt to support you through your studies, I thought. The Boss was cool; he liked football, wanted to travel to Italy and more than anything, he did not want to get married.

'Everyone thinks getting married means you've triumphed in life, but all it is is a civil state,' he had pronounced.

Downstairs, Brandy barked playfully at us.

On the way home, Marcos fell asleep on the bus seat.

'I'm not happy 'bout you hanging out with Jeno,' I told Fredy, who was carrying his cake in his hand. 'But you're all grown up now, so, just leave Marcos out of it. And when Má gets out, you're gonna have to tell her, and if she lets you keep on with it, I won't say nothing else. Just don't use weapons, Fredy, yeah? For Má's sake, don't do that.'

Fredy looked annoyed as he listened to me. 'What were you doing anyway?' he asked. 'You were in there for ages.'

I didn't know how to reply, until something hit me, a fair, serious, calm response: 'Nothing really. We just visited another planet.'

It was true.

'And what did he say 'bout Má?'

'She doesn't want to see us ... she got beaten up. She'll tell us when she's ready for us to visit.'

Fredy nodded, looking ashamed, and stared out the bus window the rest of the way home.

15

The colonia was quiet. From the avenue, I traced a path following the memories of Má's footsteps. I didn't have the phone numbers of any of the people she worked for; she knew them off by heart. She didn't save a single one just in case her phone ever fell into the wrong hands. 'You should never involve any of these people in your own problems, you hear me, mijo? They're all good people 'til they're forced to get involved,' she'd told me once, just after she'd arrived from helping out at a house round there.

It was a Sunday, the best day to find people at home. I'd skipped work at the warehouse. All the walking up and down the aisles was tiring, and it took up too much time. I needed to find a new job.

The roads in the rich-people's colonia were dead straight, no potholes, no grubby water spilling down from one side to the other. Seeing those houses, it surprised me that people needed so much space to live. I compared them with my home, my room, the roof. I'd have loved my own room to lie down in and have a rest after I got back from school, without having to hear Má or my brothers. I could put my own music on, the rebajadas by Celso Piña and la Ronda, tunes by Binomio de Oro, Luis Miguel Fuentes or some other groups, perhaps Control Machete. I wasn't particularly precious about my music, I played whatever I fancied without worrying too much about the genre, but the old tunes really got to me, the ones by Pegaso or Tropical Panamá, and sometimes some in English by AC/DC. I could have my own room to store my stuff, my schoolbooks, clothes, the old records that Papá left (music by trios like Los Panchos that I don't play any more because we've got nothing to play them on, but that I still look after carefully).

The people here had immense houses, two or three floors, with wide garages, and as many as three cars. Really? They needed all that to live? Maybe they did, but I hadn't realised because I'd got used to getting by with what we had, living with whatever fell into our hands, walking around in the clothes we had. Sometimes when I looked at those huge houses, I'd start to think that the more money you have, the more desperate you become, but it was a different kind of desperation, a desperation to have, to accumulate, to be surrounded by things that don't have any use. What did it really mean to be rich?

The houses had large gardens with neatly cut lawns and spaced-out trees, the large boughs providing plenty of shade, some pruned to look like umbrellas or fountains.

I wasn't jealous, we had the most beautiful garden in the city: our back garden was the hillside, its valleys, its trees, its caves.

I still remember the very first time I went to the top of the hill, not just up to the TV antenna where everyone goes, but right to the very top, a different summit, behind, that hardly anyone knows about. It'd been raining that week, must have been a few years back, a fine rain, like a fuzz. It was annoying cos it meant we couldn't leave the house. The filthy water splashed along the ravines, down the hillside. It was one of those days and Jeno appeared outside. The streets were still hot with persecutions and Jeno had come to say goodbye cos his mamá wanted him out of El Peñón. He arrived and whistled for me; I went outside.

'Hey, I wanna show you something,' he told me. 'Let's go up.'

'Isn't it dangerous? It's raining.'

'Nah, you just need to watch your footing. We'll skirt 'round the edge for some of it, but to get all the way up, we need to go from behind.'

I hesitated. It was around eleven in the morning, Má was out working and had taken my brothers with her. Jeno and I didn't take much with us, just a bag of oranges and a tub of chilli powder I stuffed in my trouser pocket. At first, the fog was really thin and everything looked only slightly blurry. The earth was soft, wet and dangerous. The bushes had been flattened by the weight of the water, greener than ever. As we went up, the fog became denser and denser; we could scarcely see more than five metres ahead of ourselves. I was absolutely soaked by the chipi-chipi drizzle. Further on, the trees began to grow, becoming lusher and leafier. Sometimes, I'd look up at the Cerro de la Silla from far away and it'd look like a very, very thin layer of green carpet, but up close, you could see it was all forest on the hillside, the trees hungrily covering everything, full of animals, some as big as bears.

I stopped and called out to Jeno because the fog was so much thicker. My heart started pounding, but then Jeno began to whistle. He was in front of me, and I could orientate myself off him. And there was a footpath too. How many people from the colonia must have marched along these paths to the top, flattening the grass, marking the way?

'This where they keep their stuff,' said Jeno when we reached a series of caves, their narrow entrances. 'No one comes up here to look. The chotas don't even get as far as your place so imagine them up here!'

A month after we went up there, Don Neto disappeared. There are a few different versions of the story. Some say they got him down at the bottom, while he was eating tacos. Sounds crazy but they say nobody fired a single shot. We all thought that when they went after him there'd be some awful killing spree, doing away with soldiers, women, kids, old people and everything. Who'd let themselves be taken without a single bullet being fired? They say the cops just wandered up to him and they greeted each other as always. One apparently then said to him, 'It's time, Don Neto.' According to hearsay, Don Neto didn't panic; he simply finished eating his tacos, and even left a tip – a whole wad of notes apparently – and then they put him in the truck and left. Others say the guys from the Golfo gang got him. That story says they found him down at the taco place too. Others say that when they blocked off the road, Don Neto's lookouts sneaked him out the edges, skirting right round the side of the neighbourhood. In any case, he disappeared.

After all that, the colonia went really quiet; we were all scared. Since then, nobody's seen him. Some people say they did actually kill him. Others say they didn't, that he's still out there somewhere hiding. Others are convinced the chotas have him banged up and they'll bring him out sometime when it suits them, when it all gets out of hand again. But what the chotas don't know is that once you're off the streets, you lose your power, you're smudged out. It makes you blurry, you lose your image, and the fear you once struck goes soft at the edges.

We reached the caves. Some of Jeno's compas were there looking after things. They said hi and looked at me suspiciously.

'He's a compa,' said Jeno. 'We're going up.'

'Bet,' replied one of them, bored and sitting on a tub of paint, listening to norteñas on a radio.

We left the caves behind and headed along a trail that led around the back of the hillside, slowly climbing. I've no idea how many hours we walked for, but eventually the fog began to thin. The air filled with the scent of wildflowers, wet earth, rocks, fresh bushes. And then, about one hundred metres in front of us, I could see it starting to clear while the pathway behind us was clouded in a grey mist.

'Nearly there,' Jeno encouraged.

I could barely walk because the last few metres had been the steepest, almost like we were rock climbing – I think that's what they call it when you look more like a mountain goat than a walker. We came out onto a clear plateau with just a few solitary patches of grass at the edges, and from there I could see we'd finally left the fog behind.

'Bit further, c'mon.'

And I followed him. It was sunny now. I felt it hot around me and when I was finally able to see, we were already high above our hillside. Only then did I turn round. We were near the top, but right behind the city.

'People come up from that side,' said Jeno, pointing, 'where that sign for the cable cars fell down. Everyone wants to see the city, but it's more beautiful from here.'

For the first time, I saw one of the most beautiful things I've ever seen. It was like waves in the sea, the clouds lapping serenely against the skirts of the hillside, before a swirl of air began to move them, edging them out the way to reveal a long chunk of rock like the prow of a ship, the mountain peaks and the plateau behind the hillside, before the fog returned, covering that piece of land until the air demanded its space back, revealing that stone prow once more, before the clouds returned to cover it again. From there I could see down the Huajuco valley to the south, west across to Juárez district and beyond that over towards Cadereyta, and a plane coming into land at the airport.

'They're like giants, aren't they?'

'Who?' asked Jeno, pulling out a cigarette and lighting it.

'The hills, it's like they're sleeping.'

'Nah.'

'What are they then?'

'Hills, that's all.'

We sat down and started peeling the oranges. Jeno took a few drags on his cigarette. The smoke was quickly taken away; the air up there at the top blew stronger.

'Chuck us an orange.'

I handed it over and he ate it, breaking it into segments and spitting out the seeds every few chews.

'In a while,' he said, 'there'll be a whole grove of oranges up here, you'll see. It'll be mine, and I'll be the only one who can come up here, pick 'em and plant more.'

'You crazy, Jeno.'

'Just you wait and see.' And he kept spitting out the seeds. 'Look, cabrón, look.' He stood up and started hunting for the seeds on the ground. 'Chingado,' he swore. 'I can't find 'em. Gimme some more.'

I passed him a couple more oranges and this time, without eating them, he took out all the seeds. When he'd collected enough, he poked around in the earth, before taking out his knife and making holes in the earth for the seeds. He repeated it a couple of times until they'd all gone.

'You got any water?'

'Nope.'

'Chingado,' he swore again. 'Oh well.' And he unzipped his trousers and peed straight onto the mounds of earth, a noisy yet serene stream. Then he sat back down next to me. We were silent for a few minutes, 'til we spotted an eagle gliding along one of the slopes. It was both majestic and tiny at the same time as it flew along.

'So, where you going?'

Jeno didn't turn towards me; his eyes were on the eagle.

'To stay with an aunt on the other side of the city, out east, towards Mitras. S'quiet out there.'

'You seen some ugly stuff, yeah?'

'Yeah, but that's just how it is.'

'How'd you see it?'

'What you wanna know for? Just leave it.'

'D'you know who got Luisfe? Was it Don Neto?'

Jeno's face clouded over. 'Pfffss …'

'OK, OK, I quit.'

It was hard to imagine there were people down there in the city, and that there was a colonia in that city with houses and people, and more people who carried weapons, and other people who chased them in the night, and that in that city, we were all really just cannon fodder, or at least *we* were.

'Time we headed back down. I wanna show you something else.'

We started back down, slower, more carefully. Almost on the edge where the fog began, we saw them: six white crosses bearing the names of the people buried there – two men, three women and a girl – their dates of birth and death. A failed expedition. Jeno stared at them a long while and then said we could go. I didn't ask why the crosses were important to him.

Going down was more dangerous. The fog swirled around us as soon as we started our descent: bitter and cold, narrow and firm. It didn't take long for our shoes to be covered in mud again. It was almost dark by the time we reached the caves again. We greeted Jeno's compas and carried on going. Down below everything was grey, silent and miserable. A few colonias had their lights on because of the fog.

Jeno turned to me and held out his hand in farewell. 'See ya later, cabrón. Look after yourself.'

'Bet.'

I never forgot that hike up the mountain, and I've always thought the sun is always out up there at the top, shining on Jeno's oranges. I've no idea if he remembers it, or if it means anything to him any more.

I finally found the first address. My legs shook because I felt like this whole thing was just ridiculous. I mean, what would these people actually do for us? They didn't even know us. Má was just one more machine, one of the many they had inside: washers, cookers, dishwashers, irons. There were two cars in the garage. How was I going to speak to them? What was I going to say? But I had to. I rang the doorbell. Like ten minutes later, a man appeared, the same one that had given the biscuits to my brothers. He wasn't wearing a suit or tie, just some long shorts and a Dodgers T-shirt.

'Yes?'

I introduced myself and, feeling all ashamed and that, I told him what had happened, about the lawyer and the judgement to clear Má's good name. My voice trembling, I told him that our dad had died, and that Má had got together with Miguel who wasn't a good person. I told him too much, but I only had one story to tell and a short amount of time to get my message across. And the man listened to me. He stood there, his arms like they'd fallen by his sides in surprise. He listened to me. Even though I wouldn't have believed it, the man paid attention.

16

While we were waiting for Má to finally allow us to visit her, my money worries and desperation to earn grew and grew, until one afternoon I arrived at the warehouse and handed Evaristo my notice. I needed more money more quickly. The work there was good, but the pay bad. When I told him, he looked at me a little sadly, as if he knew pressure were a bad advisor.

'Where are you going to go?'

'To be honest, I dunno. Maybe I'll go and sell stuff on the buses, or ask for work down at the crossroads, something that gives me more cash. With all due respect, the pay here's really bad.'

'I know it's not a lot, but it gives you something else.'

'Yeah? What's that?'

'Structure, hours, responsibilities. Out there you're just going to be muddling through. Are you dropping out of school too?'

I started to get angry. This fella had no reason to stick his nose in, but I kept it together.

'Nah, I can't do that. Má wouldn't let me.'

Evaristo asked me to follow him to his office. It was small with piles of stuff everywhere: papers, books, cables.

'D'you know how long it took me to become manager here?'

'Years.'

'Yes, years, but not that many, because I was *responsible*. I understand, Efraín, I really do. I'm from the Constituyentes colonia, over towards Axa Yazaki. You know where that is?'

'Yeah.'

'I studied up through high school, but there wasn't any money to go further. I took that education I'd been given and went and worked in offices – never under the sun – always looking for things that would help me up here, in my head. I married a woman like me, a slogger, patient. Four years ago, we put everything together and took out a mortgage on a house near here, in Apodaca. It's bigger than the houses we both grew up in. We may never finish paying it off, but every month the money goes out and we're content with the idea that one day it'll be ours. We don't live in luxury – people come here wearing jewellery that costs more than I earn in a month – but we've got everything we need. It's often tight, but we always get there. D'you know how people end up who give their whole lives over to physical labour? I mean, that's really what's at stake here.'

'No, I don't.'

'Life eats away at them, Efraín. They're burned by the sun, their muscles get weary. The desperation to earn money never gives sound advice, and less so when you're out on the streets.'

'But why would I want a life where I need more the whole time? Suffering from A to B. Never having money for anything.'

'Exactly, *exactly* that, because life isn't just about needing more. You can take your time. If you move slower, you get to look around at what's out there in the world. Maybe it'll take you longer to earn your money, and maybe you'll never be rich – that's true – but you can live your life your own way, not like everyone else says. Tell me, how many of the people you know have already been killed?'

'Um, yeah, loads.'

'And how many are already parents or about to become one? How many left school so they could have more time to work and have already made their million and left your colonia?'

'Well, no one, and yeah, quite a few girls with babies.'

'What about you?'

I didn't know how to reply. I wanted to earn money. I wanted enough to pay the lawyer, get Má out, finish high school and maybe start the prepa.

'You just don't understand, Evaristo, sir,' I finally said.

The man grimaced and sighed. 'Lots of kids come through here and leave soon after,' he said reluctantly, regretfully perhaps, but he wasn't in my shoes. Then he stood up, walked over to a cabinet, opened it and took out some notes. 'Here's your pay. But Efraín, don't forget, take your time, and whenever you want to come back, there's a place here for you. You've worked hard; I don't find that very often.'

Evaristo was right.

Over the next few weeks, I changed job every week. I sold newspapers, fruit at the crossroads, I helped out nearly every man in the colonia who worked. But in some ways, *I* was right too, because I earned more money out on the streets. I managed a couple of days washing windscreens at the traffic lights. You had to pay the guy in charge, we all paid him, but I was quick, and I asked permission first, so I didn't waste time cleaning the windscreen just for the driver to say no. I took great care of the pennies and worked all the hours God sent. Fredy carried on with Jeno, but I stayed out of it. At the weekends, I took Marcos to look for people who knew Má and to talk through the case with the lawyer who took the money in plastic bags without even counting it. The whole time, we waited for Má to want to see us. The man I spoke to before had given us the phone numbers of other people who knew her, so we were able to plan a route, visiting all the places she'd worked.

'Má didn't really work this hard, did she?' Marcos asked me one afternoon after we'd crossed the city to get to the

Talleres colonia to help a neighbour who was a house painter. We'd been there all day long with brushes and rollers, climbing up ladders to reach the top half of the house.

I answered yes, and then some. Má always had money, even when she said she didn't. I once asked her how much she had saved because in times gone by, the tub up on the hillside had contained more money. 'Enough for you all to study,' she answered. And she was right. Sometimes we only had enough to eat beans and tortillas, but when the time came to pay school fees, it was always there, always enough to buy the uniforms, books and everything else we needed. We'd go into town on the bus and Má would stock up, almost by the kilo, in a warehouse where they had lots of stuff on clearance.

Days passed until the Boss told us Má wanted us to visit her. We were so happy. We made plans to go and see her that very Sunday. The Boss told us we could take her some food and I remembered that Má really liked the tortillas they sold down on Eloy Cavazos Avenue, so we planned to buy some and take them with us.

In those few weeks, Fredy and I had grown even further apart. He would arrive late at night, often stinking of beer, strip off his trousers and socks and throw himself into bed. One afternoon, he arrived all beaten up, but he said nothing. I just saw him at the back of the house, his eyes opaque in the darkness while he dabbed at his wounds with a damp piece of cloth.

The day before our visit, Marcos and I went to buy the tortillas and stopped off at the flea market on the way back. I liked to look around the bit where the older folk from our neighbourhood and further afield came and laid out their tools, cables for Nintendos, the blades for liquidisers, and pliers. Marcos enjoyed it too. There were lots of little kids running around, playing at being lookouts, shooting each other with their pointing fingers held out like a pistol or sticks pretending to be AK-47s.

'Who wants to be the chota?'

'Not me, they always lose!'

'Stinky chotas.'

They'd start chasing each other until one of them fell over and the rest would pretend to finish him off at gunpoint.

'Sprinkle him!' yelled one.

'In the neck, in the neck, give it to him!' added another.

'What'll we do with the body? Dump it over there?'

'Maybe we should cook it!'

And then the smallest one would go down, curled up in a ball while the others surrounded him, pretending to sprinkle him with acid. The boy, even though he was already dead, would squirm and then, when he'd finished dying, would stand up, brush himself off and someone else would play the cop, until everyone had died and come back to life again.

It was already dark as we started making our way back home. Jeno, Fredy and a couple of others were near the bridge linking El Rancho, listening to a colombiana. It was one by Celso Piña, one of his old ones, 'Cumbia sobre el río'. The air picked up the words and brought them to me, a river of muffled sound, telling me about accordions, about arms raised in greeting to Colombia, about how to bring joy to our lives.

In the distance, over towards Cadereyta district, I watched the flames from one of the refinery chimneys. It was a clean fire, steady in the night, like it needed nothing more to exist. From the houses nearby wafted the smell of beans cooking in a pan, an aroma that followed us several metres until Marcos tugged on my arm.

'Look, Efra, look! There's someone in our house.'

I focused in on the house and he was right; there was someone there. We started climbing more quickly, taking large strides.

'Hey, hey!' we yelled.

The man realised he'd been spotted and took off, running downhill, opting for a different path near the house. We chased him, dropping the tortillas, but he was quick and agile. Marcos took a short cut to see if he could catch up. So did I. How we missed Fredy in moments like this. Off we went, bounding between the paths, dodging boulders, waste, the free-roaming pigs. The man cut along the edge of El Rancho, heading down the ravine, the same route I'd taken the day they took Má and I'd chased the patrols. From there I shouted Fredy's name, hoping he would hear me and join the chase. We ran as fast as we could, 'til we could make out his lithe figure more clearly in the night. I called his name, and Miguel, miserable and confused by my unknown voice, became disoriented and faceplanted the ground. He flipped over several times, like he was unrolling.

'Miguel's dead,' said Marcos.

When we got to him, he was just an empty sack, nothing more than flesh and bone, with shards of glass stuck in his elbows. I wanted to kill him, and with the adrenaline pumping, we'd barely reached him before I surprised myself by kicking him twice, hard in the stomach, focusing all the rage I'd been holding over the last weeks and months into my foot. Marcos stepped between us, and, with a terrified expression, he told me to stop.

'It's his fault, Marcos, it's all his fault,' I yelled, completely defeated. It was only then I realised we were both crying. Marcos because he was so scared by my reaction and me, because I thought we'd finally found a way to seek real justice; those kicks weren't even the start of it.

Not one day had gone by when we didn't think about Miguel. All of this was his fault, and what did he do? Nothing. He'd simply disappeared. And now there he was, rolling around on the ground as if he'd crawled out from it, a creature brought to life among the rocks and the rubbish, an ancient mineral being, half human, half corpse, whimpering. He let out several yelps of pains from the fall, from the buried glass splinters flowing with blood, and from my kicking.

'Look what you've done to me!' he yelled.

'You did it to us first,' I yelled back.

There was a strong breeze. Not far from us, a hen pecked at the ground as usual.

'What were you doing in our house? S'not yours any more.'

'Help me.'

We looked at each other, then went over and pulled him to his feet. The blood was running from his elbows.

'I think I've broken something,' he moaned. As he said that, I caught a whiff of the beer on his breath. He started whingeing about the glass, and pulled out the biggest bit that was buried in his elbow. Then he shook his head from side to side and I heard a bone crunching, his collar bone, perhaps. Then he belched.

'I'm sorry, boys. I just wanted to know if they'd let Leonor out. It was only a mattress.'

Marcos turned to look at me, as if *this* was the moment to give him a beating, to release all that pent-up anger.

'I was looking for my toolbox. I rented it, so I owe 'em a lot. They're looking for me.'

He'd left two boxes of tools in the house which he'd been using to work as an electrician, a tiler, mechanic, or one of the other thousands of ways he made his living, like so many other men round here. I hadn't wanted to sell them in case I needed them for work.

'It's been bad for me too. I've not been able to see anyone. Nobody's giving me any work. Word got round so I've got absolutely nothin', boys. I know I dropped her in it.' He groaned again. 'Can we at least get me sorted out? Let me clean myself up?'

Just then, a crowd gathered. I recognised them straightaway: Jeno, Fredy and the others.

'It's that scumbag,' said Fredy, pushing to the front.

Miguel's face looked tense, his skin bloody. I clenched my fists as my brother approached. It all happened very quickly. Fredy stopped, reached into his shirt, pulled out his pistol, cocked it and went to raise it as if to shoot Miguel. It was my turn to step between them.

The old man let out a whimper, a fearful sound in his throat, as if something had just switched off.

'What the hell is that? Put it down!' I scolded Fredy.

'That piece of shit ruined us! Let him pay for what he's done!'

'Fredy, chingado,' I swore. 'Put the gun down. You're not gonna kill him.'

'But that's what he deserves.'

'Put it down. PUT IT DOWN!'

'But, Friar … seriously?! No way, no *frickin'* way!'

'C'mon, we're gonna hand him over to the cops. Fredy, put it down.'

Jeno walked over to Fredy, put his hand on the gun and took it out of his grip.

'Let's go. This their business,' he ordered the others.

Fredy finally collapsed and Miguel heaved a sigh of relief.

'I'm sorry, boys,' he started to murmur. 'All I wanted was to do what your jefa wanted, but idiot that I am, I took the easy way out. People've nicked mattresses like that before. Didn't think it'd all blow up like this. And look at me now, I'm screwed as well as you. We're all screwed!'

I turned to look unwillingly at Miguel.

'See, thing is, our jefa's in jail, and you're not. We gonna take you and hand you in,' I told him.

We walked him down to his mother's house. She was outside with her sons. It was the same scene as before. They were all sitting in rocking chairs, or normal chairs, with a beer at their feet, taking in the night air.

A summary of a recent football match was playing on a radio inside. Miguel cleared himself a space among his brothers, who wasted no time asking what the hell had happened.

'I fell on my way down, that's what happened.'

'Ay, mijito, my son,' cried his mama. 'Let me clean you up.'

The old lady stood up and went inside. When she returned, she was carrying a ragged cloth and some alcohol and she set about using them to clean her son's wounds. Miguel moaned every time the damp rag touched his elbows and his knees where his mamá was carefully removing the shards of glass. One of his brothers handed him a beer and Miguel took a few gulps before handing it back. He looked skinnier than ever, bonier. He'd aged in those months.

'Señora,' I addressed his mamá, 'now you *can* help us. We just need Miguel to go to the cops and say it was him that nicked the mattress. That way they'll release our mamá.'

The lady carried on cleaning her son's wounds. She didn't answer.

Marcos tugged on my shirt.

'Are you crazy? My son's not gonna do any of that. If they bang him up, how the hell we gonna get him out?'

I stood there frozen to the spot. The brothers looked shiftily at one another; a couple took another swig from their beers. They were completely mummified, their eyes fixed on the old woman cleaning the wounds.

'The lazy donkey should've gone for his tools earlier, but he left it to the last minute.'

'But, Señora ...'

'Don't you *Señora* me, remember, we all get on as best we can. Now, get lost.'

'We're gonna talk to the police,' said Fredy.

'You talk to them and I'll tell everyone I saw your mother helping you up the hill with that mattress. Now, piss off.'

I wanted to spit at her. I wished I had a machine gun like Jeno's so I could do away with everyone right there and then. Five hundred bullets, just like those kids had been playing before.

'Get lost, and forget you were ever here. Useless kids.'

'Yeah, yours,' shot back Fredy.

The men laughed. 'Those the kids who wanted to be all educated, eh, Miguel?' asked one of the brothers, and with a smirk – of shame, or of mocking, I wasn't quite sure which – Miguel nodded.

We started back up the path towards home. Although Miguel hadn't been able to get in, the padlock and chain on the door were almost bust. I couldn't stop looking at Fredy; his anger, weariness and desperation were bristling. I picked up the tortillas that had been scattered across the floor; some were already supper for the ants.

'Don't go doing anything stupid,' I warned him eventually, as he headed off back down the hill.

'Nah, but that old man can go to hell.'

Inside me, I could feel my rage. It was the ugliest emotion I'd ever felt, all because of Miguel, his mamá, the five hundred bullet wounds. As Fredy left and I heard his footsteps head downhill, I knew exactly where he was going and what he was going to do. But Jeno owed me one; he had my brother. He was my only hope and that's why I texted him. A short message, telling him how he was paying. He answered with a simple 'K'.

Later that night we heard shooting. The news reached us the next morning: Miguel's mamá's house had been smoked. Nobody had been killed, but the message was clear. As we left to go to the prison, I felt the eyes of the colonia following us. At El Rancho Jeno was eating some tacos de barbacoa. Fredy was with him and as soon as he saw us, he came over. I nodded as I saw them, and using his fingers, Jeno gestured shooting into the air. *Pum, pum, pum*, the shots rang in my head. *Pum, pum, pum.* The bullets. Then he sent me a message.

It said, 'We're even.'

17

The visiting room was small, barely more than a few concrete tables occupied by other people. It was our first visit to see Má so the Boss came with us, that and so he could tell us what would happen next with her defence. He had good news, he said. It seemed that the courts had accepted this special type of judgement. While it was unusual here in Mexico, it was apparently laid out in some Magna Carta or other. We'd brought along some food, some tacos de barbacoa we'd bought at the prison entrance, along with some orange juice and the rescued wheat tortillas. But the guards had poked around in the tacos during our security check, and they forced us to drink the orange juice. They were checking to make sure we weren't smuggling any contraband. The tacos with the shredded tortillas didn't look particularly appetising – they looked like someone had puked them up – but we still took them through to her.

Fredy seemed uneasy in there. Something was up, I could tell. We were almost like complete strangers now. At one point when we were younger, I'd tried to get on with him, but we'd never been close. He'd had his compas and they used to play at chotas and narcos out on the bare hillside. School was too much of an effort for him, and it seemed like too much of an effort to talk to me as well, although I can't say I tried very hard either. Me being the older brother and my way of being 'the eldest' seemed to bug him. He went through a phase of playing video games in the stores, and he'd sold newspapers in the afternoons, but nothing had driven us apart like these few months and our two different approaches to dealing with Má's imprisonment.

I didn't even ask about the shooting at Miguel's mother's. Out the corner of my eye, I could see he was worried. He stood awkwardly at the entrance as he went through the security check, and now his eyes flicked from one window to the other, and then back to the guarded door. Marcos, perhaps because he was still that bit younger, didn't find the situation strange at all. Yes, Má was a prisoner, but that was all.

'Calm down, Fredy,' I said to him. 'It'll all be over soon.'

'Could've finished it all ages ago.'

The lawyer listened to us, his hands in his pockets, looking a bit bored. At ten o'clock, the prisoners were brought out, although there weren't many. Even though the room was full, there must have been inmates whom nobody visited.

'The women tend to get forgotten pretty quickly,' Raúl had said. 'They just leave them here.'

Má was one of the first. She ran to see us and hugged us. She smelled of soap and her hair was damp. She'd aged loads, as if the years had suddenly caught up with her in there. I noticed grey hairs she didn't have before, extra wrinkles on her chin. Her body had just generally deteriorated. Marcos was so happy to see her he cried. He was the first to be hugged, followed by Fredy – who tensed – and then me. How strange it felt to hug Má, to feel her warmth, to feel her close. It was rare for her to hug us or ruffle our hair; she'd always been distant in that way. With her it was always 'do, do, do', always in a hurry, scurrying around. She offered almost no tender gestures at all, but we knew she loved us. Má started to cry, but then she dried her tears with her hands. She turned to the lawyer and said, 'Señor Morcillo, thank you for coming.'

Nobody mentioned how long it had taken for her to let us see her, she'd taken her time. It had been tough for all three of us, but Marcos most of all. He was happy to be with Má, you could see it in his eyes, in the way he looked at her, as if Má was an apparition.

'No worries at all, Señora Leonor. It's a pleasure.'

We sat down at one of the tables that Marcos had pulled over. Around us, what we'd just experienced was being repeated.

'We brought you some food,' said Marcos, and held out the polystyrene tray with the dark mess of meat that Má began to eat, hurriedly, without noticing that they weren't really tacos at all.

'They're delicious, mijos, thank you so much.'

We let her eat in silence and, when she was finished, since we had no napkins, she wiped her hands on the edge of the chair so she didn't get her uniform dirty.

'We saw Miguel last night, Má. He tried to get in the house,' Fredy told her.

Má tensed as she heard his name. The room pressed down on me and I couldn't breathe. The light blurred.

'What did he want?'

'His tools. He'd left 'em behind.'

'Let him have them, so he has no reason to come back again,' she ordered.

'We avenged you, Má,' Fredy continued.

'What do you mean?'

Fredy turned to me, and I shook my head, thinking, *Don't do it, you fool.*

'Jeno helped us out, gave his family a good scare.'

Má was petrified. I saw her lose her calm tranquillity. It wasn't a chain reaction like in the movies, but something much slower, a continual change, rippling over her skin, draining the blood from her face. Then she grabbed hold of Fredy's wrists and with a contained rage she implored him,

'Don't get involved with those people, please. I've given my whole life to keep you far away from them.'

'But they're the only ones who can defend us, Má,' my brother replied.

Má's hand gripped my younger brother's wrists even tighter. 'What've you been up to, Alfredo?' She rarely called him that. 'The other day they told me someone on the outside was protecting me. I thought it might have been Miguel, I don't know, maybe even you, Efraín, what with you hanging around with that Jeno. Was it you, Alfredo? Tell me the truth.'

Fredy held his head up and nodded.

The lawyer finally interrupted. 'Could someone please explain to me what's happening?'

'Nothing, Boss, my brother's stuff, but nothing that'll affect us,' I said.

'We can't let *anything* affect it. Señora Leonor, if they find out that you're working, or that you've worked with, people who – let's just say, aren't such a positive influence on your case – even if it's just for a day or two, it'll be so much harder for us. We're basing this whole case on your innocence, and on the fact there's no witnesses linking you to the robbery, no security guards or anyone else on the way back home. On the fact that your name is clean.'

'I'm not involved with anyone, I'm clean.' Má turned to us. 'What about you, can you boys say the same?'

This time, Fredy didn't raise his head. Marcos looked completely lost in the whole conversation.

'That's how it needs to stay,' said the Boss. 'Don't get involved with anything. What we have to do now is wait, hold your nerve. Do what the guards, or the officers, tell you to do. If you have to go hungry, or eat whatever they give you, eat only that. We've made good progress with this judgement to clear your good name. It's untried in the state, but I've found a judge who's willing to take it on. And it's going well with the interviews and the witnesses, isn't it, Efraín?'

The lawyer looked at me and I nodded. We'd spent a few weekends visiting the houses in the neighbourhoods where Má had worked. I told her about the men and women who wanted to help. I didn't mention the ones that didn't. Among them was one lady who spoke really badly about Má, said she'd seen Má pinch a small gold chain we'd never even seen. The woman hadn't been in a good frame of mind, she'd seemed annoyed and hadn't been pleased to see us.

At the start, we'd done well collecting testimonies, but it had tailed off after that. Some of Má's employers were really surprised by the news and then looked at us as if *we* were the ones in jail. There was one woman – I remember her well – who once she found out why we were there, pulled her front door to so we couldn't see anything inside, as if we were there scouting the place out to see what we could nick. But we had five witnesses. One was even a lawyer who had said he'd get in touch with the Boss to help and had actually followed through. I held much faith in the judgement.

We spent the rest of the two hours chatting about what Má had been doing inside. She told us the prison was like a small village, there were several restaurants, a movie theatre, stalls that sold all sorts of things. The guards controlled everything, because, unlike the male prisons where the prisoners were in charge, the narco women who were caught and the normal prisoners tended to lead quieter lives. Not that this guaranteed it was all completely peaceful, of course.

Before we left, Má took Fredy aside and said something to him. From the looks of it, it wasn't something he enjoyed hearing. Then Má began to cry and hugged my brother more tightly, as if she was saying goodbye to him. I felt all weird inside because maybe Fredy had just told her he was a lookout, maybe he'd broken Má's heart, and despite her best efforts, she'd be unable to save one of her sons. Fredy came back to us all serious and we finally left. The lawyer told us he'd drop us back in his car, and once we'd climbed in, he asked us to tell him the truth.

'If the courts find out you're involved in something underhand, even though it's rare for them to go digging in cases like these, it'll offroad everything we're doing and you can kiss goodbye to your mamá for ever. They could send her down for at least ten years for stealing a mattress. That company is huge and they're demanding the maximum term. It's ridiculous but I've seen people rot in jail for nothing more than stealing a mouthful of bread.'

I turned to face Fredy whose anger seemed to have drained away. 'Thing is,' I said, 'there's people from El Golfo in the colonia.'

'The drugs cartel?'

'Yeah.'

'And do you boys know them?'

'Hell, Boss, we all know 'em,' I replied. 'We all know people who sell and traffic. And they're not all bad people. They just do their business and leave. They don't all go round killing. They don't—'

'And what happened with this Miguel person?'

'He tried to break into our house, so we chased him. He fell over and we took him down to his house. We thought he'd hand himself in, but his jefa told us he wouldn't. Fredy got angry and went with Jeno—'

'What did they do?' Raúl was shaking his head.

'Well, they fired a load of bullets at their house,' I finally said, ashamed.

What a strange sensation I felt. Our whole lives we'd tried to keep out of all this, or rather, not get drawn into it. We hadn't asked for help from anyone. We'd tried to stand on our own two feet. But we'd failed. It was impossible to stay out of it. Only one girl had ever managed it. She was a secretary now and no longer met up with anyone from the colonia. Every morning she'd leave home all done up. When it rained, she used to put plastic bags over her feet, carrying her shoes round her neck. Once she was out of the mud, she would put them on again. She found a partner, but never brought him back to the colonia. When she got married, her mamá, Señora Eladia, was so happy, but then we realised her daughter never came back. Señora Eladia spent the next few years adopting cats. She died alone. All they found was the dead bodies of her cats in the patio of her house, and that's where the rumour grew from that she was a witch. Má made us study. She'd put a roof on the house, kept her home clean, and she saved up to buy what we needed for school.

'You dumbass kids,' Raúl eventually said. 'I understand, but from now on, you've *got* to keep a low profile. Let us take care of it. And stay away from Jeno. I'll speak to him – he's my client too, after all.'

That made Fredy react. 'Don't do that, Boss. I'll speak to him.'

We went back home, and once we got to El Rancho, we found everyone sitting there, listening to music. Fredy stopped and looked at me, kind of embarrassed, and said, 'I'm staying here.'

'What? Here? C'mon, let's go up.'

'No, Efra, I'm staying here. I'm big enough to make my own mind up. I'm not quitting school, but this is where I'm hanging out. I know you told Jeno not to let me do what I wanted to do. It's cool. Thanks for looking out for me, but now stop. From now on, I decide.'

I looked at Jeno who came over and greeted my brother like one of the gang. It was like he could read my thoughts.

'I'll look out for him,' he said. 'Nothing's gonna happen to him, and anyway, you need the money for the lawyer. He's a compa, but one of these days, others are gonna want to make you pay. And your jefa can rest easy too, no one's gonna touch her. You think that's easy to sort out in there?'

My brother went with them and as he started to say hi to the others, a knot formed in my throat. Marcos and I left Fredy there and continued the walk back home. Fredy popped home at about three. He had a piece of roast chicken. I didn't want it, but Marcos ate it for dinner.

'When Má gets out, I'll get out too. Word.'

'No one ever gets out,' I told him.

I was right.

18

I didn't sleep that night. I felt so utterly helpless. I couldn't change the way of things. I thought about Evaristo, the warehouse and everything he'd told me. *Go calmly*, he'd said. *Look around, take in the view.* Some horizon I had before me. I was reaching the end of high school and my compas were already looking around for jobs. Lots of them had already found something, selling food – fries or elote – or else looking after businesses. Others planned to try the big factories, while others dreamed of driving a truck and seeing the country.

Me, I didn't exactly know what I wanted to do. Until just a few months ago, I'd wanted to keep studying, go on to the preparatoria for the next two years. I'd even requested the registration forms for the prepa nearby, the one down near La Pastora, part of the university. It was a huge school with tall three-storey buildings and an enormous concrete yard. And yet, I'd felt rejected. The security guard made me wait ages before I could go in and ask for the forms. The students all looked the same in identical clothing. This wasn't my world either.

So I'd looked at one of the Conalep technical colleges instead. It looked like it had a bigger mix of people, people who looked like me, but I didn't like what they had to offer – polymers and mechanics – although they did have one course that looked sick: aircraft manufacturing and glider maintenance, but it was a lot of hours and a lot of maths, and worse still, it wasn't on offer here in Monterrey.

Fredy arrived gone four in the morning, skinny as he was, but stinking of cigarettes. He went to get into bed. Clumsily he took off his trousers and put on the shorts he slept in. As his clothes fell to the floor, there was a heavy clunk, and it wasn't long before he was snoring. I was on the other side of the room, having retreated to the foam mat as always. I got up and quickly found his gun, a pistol, small but functional. I grabbed it and took it over to the window. I opened the magazine and it was full: eight clean bullets, cold in the barrel. With those bullets he could kill someone. Or defend himself. The air coming from the upper hillside was cooler now and the showery season would start soon. The heat that had been flogging the city had begun to disappear little by little. What would it feel like to shoot? A shot is the same the world over: an explosion that kills. I looked again at my sleeping brother.

I took out all of the bullets, looked closely at them and then replaced them. *To protect you*, I told him silently. It was all I could do as his brother. I imagined that, just as there would be an orange tree up on the northern summit, I'd just sown a gunpowder tree with gunpowder roots, whose fruits would be bullets and cartridges. Tree after tree would cover the slopes, reaching down as far as the first houses and spreading their roots into the neighbourhood.

The next day when I woke up, Fredy had already gone and Marcos was sitting on the chair. It was school holidays so we had no classes. I went to the door and looked at the city in the distance, cloaked in a white haze, a plane starting its descent towards the airport. I cooked scrambled eggs with salsa for Marcos, ate half and as we descended the hill, Jeno and the others were already up and about at El Rancho. They were drinking colas and eating tacos for breakfast. Jeno whistled to me, and I whistled back.

I waved as we left and headed downhill. Monday seemed quiet. We were going to look for the last person we needed. Our steps were firm as we walked down to the avenue and waited for the bus. As we got on, it was really empty, so we sat wherever we wanted.

The *run-run* of the engine was singing a lullaby. I was looking at the adverts, reading them as we went past: Kindergarten Fomerrey 20; Exhausts and Engines Ramírez; Tarot card reading; Mary's Tortillas; Health Foods San José; Automotive mechanics: Computer diagnostics – don't be taken in; Tortas Las Tortugas; Modelorama agency; Locks and Lifts; GRILLED MEAT, ROAST POTATOES; R-85 Rancho Tequila; Famsa Bank – We're part of your best efforts; Sherwin-Williams Decorating now open; Fecomsa Hardware Store; Berel Paints: vinyls, enamels, textured; Dental Corporation: 83-60-30-48 braces only $169; Sport-Gym-Zumba. And alongside these ads, people. People sitting on the benches at bus stops; old men with worn hats; podgy women carrying little kids in their arms; abandoned, empty houses; piles of waste; graffitied tags from different gangs – the Burócratas and Sin Nombre 54, the Lomas de la Silla and the Nuevo Almaguer, El Peñón and the Arboledas; telephone masts; and water tanks with their worn and dirty cement walls. Pawn shops; more gyms; and sad-looking dental practices; the Lobo trading house, where almost all the old folk and some of the neighbourhood men came to sell what they'd picked up in the streets or bought from their pick-ups shouting, 'Any old iron'.

I decided to close my eyes and orientate myself purely from the coming and going of the bus along the avenue. I knew where it stopped, where it changed lanes into town, where it went up and over a bridge, where it entered a narrow street to avoid a bumpy road, and that's where we got off, so we could board another bus to the Contry colonia.

When we got there, we wandered along the streets feeling a bit lost until we reached a broad avenue with a central reservation of trees and grass. On the porch of one house, a slender woman was shaking her hands at another woman, a woman like Má, plump, hair tied back, clothes like ours, holding some huge bags in her hands that she clearly had to load into the car. We were walking past just as she came out. The effort of carrying the bags made her stumble and we could hear the sound of breaking glass.

'You broke them, Aracely,' the slender woman yelled.

Marcos ran over to help her up which made her start screaming. 'Go away, go away!' And then, in full desperation, she cried, 'Oh! Mijo, son, help! Help!'

Marcos stood there paralysed, and the other woman, Aracely, quickly got to her feet. I went over as fast as I could and pulled my brother away. A boy about my age came out the house, frightened and skinny. He was wearing blue jeans and a colourful T-shirt with Iron Man on the front. He looked at us fearfully and I could see his arm trembling.

'Help me, mijo! This boy just came running over, call the police!'

Marcos turned to me and as he did so, the other woman, Aracely, tried to calm her employer down.

'He was just trying to help, Doña Luisa, that's all.'

'Well, why did he have to get involved? You! Go and call the police!'

I looked angrily at the boy. I tugged Marcos and we started to run in the opposite direction, as fast as we could.

My legs were buckling beneath me. I didn't even know why we were running. Marcos was behind me. We finally came to a park and we hid on a bench. Just then, a man walking his dog looked at us suspiciously and clear as anything, I heard him take out his phone and call the police, so I pushed Marcos, and we started walking again, more slowly this time, sweating buckets.

'But we didn't do anything, Efra.'

'Why d'you get involved?'

'We were only on the street.'

'It was *their* street.'

'But—'

'But nothing.'

A few streets further on the patrol found us. The cops put on the siren as soon as they spotted us. Our hands were empty. All I had on me was some money, a few notes I'd earned over the last few weeks, money I was planning to give to the lawyer.

'Hey, what were you little warts doing in Saturno?'

So that was the name of the street.

'Nothing, sir. We were just passing through and my brother went to help a lady that had fallen over.'

'Get in, cabrones. We'll see what the lady has to say.'

'But we didn't do anything.' Marcos started to cry.

'Look at that, all big and tough to start with, but they soon turn into cry-babies,' said one of the chotas with a smile.

We climbed in the cops' pick-up, and they took us back to the woman's house, but there wasn't anyone there any more. The house was all locked up, the gate too. Not even the car was there. The officer sounded the siren again, but nobody appeared. Then he climbed out and rang the bell. Still nothing. Eventually, Aracely appeared and without opening the gate, she said that her boss had gone to play cards with her friends. The officer looked annoyed. He muttered and turned to his colleague. When he got back to the vehicle, I heard him mutter, 'Ridiculous people.'

They turned on the engine and headed out of this neighbourhood and into another, the one that Jeno and I had cut through the day they took Má. They kicked us out, but not before going through our pockets. The chotas took all the money I had on me.

'What are you scummy kids doing messing around in this neighbourhood, anyway?' sneered the officer. 'Better to stick with what you know, eh.'

They drove off leaving us there with absolutely nothing. Marcos was frightened. We were about fifteen kilometres from home, plus the hill. We'd never walked that far. I knew the avenue from coming and going on the bus, but up until then, I hadn't walked it. I remembered what Evaristo said: taking it slowly means you can see other things; a life at a different speed gives you a rhythm where other stories can fit in; make time and space for other people to show up, to observe the finer details of people, the streets, the houses.

That day I discovered things I'd never noticed, like a line of trees with purple flowers, and the names of some of my compas above the gates of several businesses. In one place they were grilling meat, a man moving the meat from one side of the hotplate to the other. Some girls my age were balancing on tiptoe as they rocked to and fro on a rocking chair. Nobody was chasing anyone.

I started chatting to Marcos and he told me how he'd been feeling during this whole episode. I told him about the time when he was little when he'd got lost on the hillside and how worried Má had been. He told me how much more scared he was when he went into a different colonia. We were just two brothers walking home, chatting along the city's streets.

Fredy came back up that afternoon. He was happy. He had a pork torta in a paper bag that'd got wet at the edges.

'What is it?' he asked when he saw my disturbed look.

'The feds stopped us earlier,' I replied. 'Over in Contry.'

'You should've called us.'

'Nah, it's fine.'

'Jeno and me would've come.'

'They took all our money and we've not eaten all day. Marcos is starving.'

'Have the torta, here, take it.'

'Come back to us, Fredy,' I begged him.

I hoped he would give it up, hand back his gun and stay at home. He laughed. Then he asked me about Papá. He could barely remember him, or so he said.

'I do,' I answered. I shared an old memory about this place here, when he first built the house, a time when I watched him dance with Má. And how they had both jumped when they saw Papá had a tarantula on his hand.

Fredy laughed out loud.

Night fell. He was twelve years old. All grown up. Grown up enough to handle a pistol. Grown up enough to roam to the very edges of the colonia. He ran back downhill.

He ran.

19

Two days later they came for Jeno and anyone that was with him. Nobody fired a shot. The Grand Marquis stayed where it was, parked up in El Rancho, doors open, the radio playing *La Caliente*.

Or so they say.

20

The judge entered the room and asked us to be seated. It wasn't like in the American movies where there's a witness stand with the defendant, their lawyer and the prosecution all sitting on the same level, as if they all had the same approximation to the law. No. Here the room was small and jam-packed with desks with several people working away at them. Women came and went with papers. To one side, there was a narrow passageway with bars all the way around which led to some cells where the prisoners were held.

Señor Raúl was at the other end to this grille, the lawyer from the mattress company too. He was very well dressed and greeted Raúl politely; the Boss had told me they'd been classmates during their training. When Má appeared, my heart started pounding. Being the eldest, I was the only one of us there thanks to special permission that the lawyer had been granted.

'The defendant is accused of the aggravated theft of a luxury mattress in March of this year, property of the company Súper Camas S. A. de C. V., henceforth, the Prosecution. Mattress model: Estefanía, product code: 2389. The Prosecution is demanding the maximum penalty for this case, which carries between ten and fifteen years in prison,' announced the judge. 'The stolen object was discovered by police officers in the region of hillside IV, in the suspect's abode in an unnamed road in the colonia Gloria Mendiola, following a search warrant granted by this jurisdiction.'

The judge's words piled up, one of top of the other, obstinate and difficult. She summarised everything that had happened that day: Má's arrival at the local jail and her subsequent transfer to the women's prison. The Boss listened in silence and took notes. He was there with two other lawyers he'd introduced to us just that day, two young men who were doing *pro bono* work for a civil organisation, so they said. The lawyer for the company listened calmly to the case, and when the judge requested witnesses to be called, I pricked up my ears and eyes. There must have been people who saw us taking that mattress up Montes Azules Road – the Boss had predicted this – but who would have remembered it?

They did have witnesses.

A woman we'd never seen before entered the room, sat down close to the judge and leaned into the microphone. She introduced herself as a long-standing resident of the neighbourhood, who lived on Montes Azules.

'Do you recognise this lady?' the company's lawyer asked her.

'Vaguely. She lives with *Los Salvajes*, The Wild Ones.'

'Who, or what, are *The Wild Ones*?'

'They're the ones who live right at the top, up on the hillside where the road ends. Thieves, scroungers, bad people, tough nuts, the sort of people that rob you in the market, who live for the day. People not to be trusted.'

'And in this particular case, do you remember having seen this lady transporting this item along the road on the fourteenth of March of this year?'

'Yes, Your Honour. She carried it up the road, helped by her children.'

Hearing this, Má turned to look at us. She looked emotionally drained.

The Boss glanced at me and gestured encouragingly.

'How did they transport it?' the company lawyer wanted to know.

'They dragged it up the road; it was very sad to see because I could see just how beautiful that mattress looked, all clean and comfortable. I imagine by the time it got up there it was all battered and dirty.'

'And how long did it take them?'

'Probably about an hour because they passed in front of my house at about four o'clock and when I left a little while later, they hadn't got very far.'

'And you recognise this lady as the person carrying most of the item's weight?'

'Yes, sir. It was her.'

The silence seized my body, and I could hear only the beating of my heart. More witnesses came forward, some saying they had seen Má down at the factory watching what time the goods vehicles came in and out. I didn't know Má sometimes used to go and meet Miguel as he came out of work so they could spend time together, eating tacos, or browsing the clothes and handbags at the Soriana supermarket. There were photos of Má outside the mattress factory. People from the warehouse came forward as well as the officers who had confiscated the mattress. Inside, fear and anger were eating me up because desolation had devoured everything else. Back home in the colonia, nobody knew where Fredy, Jeno or the others were, and when I asked, people replied that I already knew.

'Why are you doing this to yourself?' Isra from the store had asked me.

When it was finally the Boss's turn to speak, he whispered something to the other lawyers. What he said next is stored firmly in my mind. It's here, always to hand, because I never want to forget it.

'Sometimes, even if justice does not exist, the truth does. People can lie and get away with it, but the truth is impossible to hide. It is the backdrop of everything we do.

It goes beyond the relationships we make. It is unique and untransferable.'

The Boss spoke about injustice, saying that bad things happened to people like us, and that people could invent stories in exchange for a few coins. In the age of technology, everything, evidence – videos and text messages – was corruptible, he said, because injustice didn't need to make an effort. Society had created its own enemies a long time ago, an army of invisible beings, placing the weight of the world's apparent evil on the people who had the least.

Then he started talking about a book. He said that Má was a Jean Valjean of our age, that we were like Cossette, devoid of any real way to lift ourselves out of our own poverty, other than by working hard. And while many of us were part of criminal gangs and even if a class existed that was dedicated to theft and exploitation, those men and women did not fully represent those at the top of their society. That was what he said: *those at the top*. He said that among them were people of honour, people for whom honest work was their greatest possession.

And he named Má, citing her nearly twelve years of uninterrupted work in the city, public holidays included, working in the houses where she was employed. Some Christmases and New Years, Má would arrive home after midnight with food that her bosses had given her after their parties had almost finished and she had finally been allowed to leave. Sometimes the women would send Má home in a taxi (not all people with money are mean) and we'd go and wait for her at the bus stop down on the avenue. And the four of us would walk slowly, while all around us there was fiesta, barbecues, music blaring from almost all the houses, Colombian vallenatas and rebajadas. And once home, Má would rummage through the pots she'd been given, taking out a little chicken in achiote, rosemary, fish, spaghetti, apple salad, bread. Raúl stated that during that whole time, all of these people had opened the doors of their houses to Má, revealing their prized possessions, their intimate lives, their clothes, their grief. Má – quiet and diligent – had not only respected this extra intimacy but had driven these qualities into her sons who were hard working and who had been able to cover their legal costs by working not only in the streets, but wherever and however they could. He skilfully related my labours of selling tacos, cleaning chairs, my work in the damaged goods warehouse. He told of Fredy working at the grocer's with Marcos helping out, and that the mattress, although it had been found in our house, had arrived by alternative ways, with lies.

The judge listened attentively. 'So, who stole the mattress and took it there?'

Raúl named Miguel, and described every step of what had happened, contradicting the witness testimonies, and offering other evidence instead, including the photographs of the beating I had received from the police when they came into our home.

'This case is not to prove the culpability of the guilty party, but rather to demonstrate her palpable innocence through her good name – as proven by our witnesses – and to refute once and for all the evidence presented against my client by the company – both falsely and badly documented, or including wholly fictious stories, as I have demonstrated – and thus she should receive justice from this tribunal and maintain her innocence outside of prison.'

The lawyer for the mattress company crossed his arms. They began to file in, all the people that we knew would speak well of Má. Her employers, women from the rich neighbourhoods who seemed to come from some other planet, people who had nothing to do with us at all. Together they created a list of good deeds, facts that placed into doubt all the bad actions she was said to have done. Má shed a few tears as one lady gave evidence – they hadn't always got on, I found out later. When our witnesses finished, a ball of ice formed in my throat, and a harpoon dragged me into the courtroom.

The mattress lawyer called for a witness: Miguel's mother. The broad matriarch strode forwards. What on earth had just happened? It appeared that the woman hadn't just sat there twiddling her thumbs after Jeno's people had fired at her house, and she'd shown up to give information in the case against Má. And that was absolute gold for the company's lawyer.

The woman came to the front and introduced herself. She said where she lived and explained how she had met Má: Má was a prostitute who had fallen in love with her son, Miguel Saldívar. Má had asked him for a mattress so they could 'roll around in it', her very words.

'And her kids aren't saints either. The two older ones are mixed up in the local gangs, they're thugs involved with the drugs cartel that operates round there. And if they want to come for me after all this, I'm not frightened. I hope that woman rots in jail for what she's done. Although perhaps it's better for her she doesn't get out, not now they've disappeared her middle one.'

Má paled, not so much because of the statement by Miguel's mother – I guess she'd been expecting something like that – but because of those last few words. Raúl and I had decided not to tell Má about Fredy, so she didn't come into the trial worked up and defeated.

It was Raúl who spoke next. 'Your Honour, if I may? What has just happened is a clear example of what I presented in my introduction to this case, how quickly lies, anger and personal quarrels come out when faced with truth and justice. Here we are, here *you* are, perhaps now doubting everything that has been said in the last hour about my client's good name. A cloud has come to darken the day. And yet it does nothing more that indicate that my client has not only been unjustly imprisoned – there is no further evidence other than reinterpretations by this unconvincing evidence, nor witnesses whose statements are any more conclusive – but her human rights have also been infringed. She was taken from her home with no prior arrest warrant; the document you have in front of you is dated the day *after* my client was arrested. She was transferred to prison in record time and afterwards incarcerated in Social Readaptation Centre number five. What we want to highlight here is that it is *good* people who receive the worst injustices, simply for belonging to a certain social group. We believe individuality exists beyond the social class structure. This ought not be cast into doubt by the revenge of certain people who come here to lie. In the annexed evidence I have given to you, it is documented how Señor Miguel Saldívar arrived at Montes Azules Road in a pick-up truck with the mattress in it. He climbed out of the vehicle and began his ascent up the hillside with the item. What the prosecution has presented is unfounded evidence, designed to blame an innocent person with the aim of ensuring that somebody, *anybody*, pays for this crime. And that is not justice. And moreover, that is not truth.'

The judge listened to those words and reviewed the documents. She took some notes and announced that the outcome would be presented in a couple of weeks. Raúl and the *pro bono* lawyers were not particularly happy as the judge left the room.

'Who was that woman?' demanded Raúl.

'The mother of Má's boyfriend,' I replied.

'She's put us in a hole. Go home. Stay out of trouble. Please. Any word about your brother?'

I shook my head.

The hillside had swallowed them, so they said on the street.

21

One week later, what had been predicted to happen, happened: the Zozaya cartel arrived in the colonia. It was night-time. After several weeks of testing the waters, they arrived one Saturday, in the early hours, just as the last few people in El Rancho were gathering their things and heading home. I'd been to say thank you to the people that had testified on Má's behalf. It wasn't much; I just introduced myself and thanked them for having given up their time to defend her. Some of them asked if what Raúl had said about Miguel was true and I nodded. 'I hope they find him,' they repeated. Marcos was with me.

On the way back, we searched for Fredy. As we passed any small groups we asked after him, but nobody knew anything. Even just seeing us made them nervous. I now think having siblings is a strange thing. You're born from the same mother or father, you live so much of your life with them, but you soon begin to follow your own routes and pathways, your own dreams, your own ways of problem solving. And then one day, when they've been by your side your whole life, they just disappear. They're taken away, they go. And the brother you had will never be that again. He will live on in your memory, and nothing more. The phrase, 'If only ...' becomes an uncertain future. Maybe Fredy resisted, maybe he escaped. But deep down, I knew. *I hope he was lucky in death.* I hope.

The last Friday before the case closed, I took the book *Les Misérables* out of the school library. I had discovered it was there and I decided I would try to read it. it was the book with that character the Boss had referred to. I stuck it in the woven backpack I had with me and then took Marcos with me to the Boss's office to see if there was any news. Estrella was there again, bored and playing on her phone. She spotted me and beamed at me, but I was feeling down. To me it felt as if she was miles away, like she belonged to a whole different life. She told me her uncle was with some clients, but she stood up and knocked on the door to let him know we were waiting. She came straight back and told me there hadn't been a decision yet. Then the lawyer came out and said he might be a while.

'Can I go?' Estrella asked.

The Boss looked annoyed, but he said yes; she just needed to make sure she'd locked up properly on the way out. We left at the same time, and were about to say goodbye when she stood there looking at us, and said, 'Do you want another coffee?'

Marcos turned to me and nodded.

'But we'll pay for ours.'

'Fine, whatever. Come on.'

We didn't go far this time. When we got there, we stopped still. We weren't dressed for somewhere like that. I was wearing a washed-out T-shirt and old trainers.

'They're gonna think we're there to nick something. Probably best we don't go in.'

'Come on, no one's going to think that.'

Marcos shot me a stubborn look.

I gave in. 'At least it won't be so hot inside.'

'What do you want?' Estrella asked us once we were inside.

I turned to my brother. It struck me how calm he looked after our last experience at the bookshop. And I thought about Fredy who would perhaps never get to be in a place like this because we were barred from entering – like so many other shops, nightclubs, cafes, cinemas, spaces where people like us never went – not because we didn't fit in, but because we ourselves had decided that this other indoor space was out of bounds, because our territory was elsewhere: the streets, the fields, the schools, the gyms where there's not much there, the technical colleges, tacos at weekends, second-hand clothes, the Fundadores market where they sell everything really cheap.

'What would you recommend for my brother?'

Estrella looked at him. 'Do you want something hot or cold?'

Marcos asked me for permission with his eyes. 'Cold.'

'With coffee or without?'

'Without.'

'Well, you could order from this board here.'

In the end, he chose a vanilla *frappe*.

It was like a milkshake, only different. It was so cold. I ordered the same. We sat on a bench, but I noticed the guy next to us shield his laptop from us and tighten his grip on his backpack.

'Did you read the book?' Estrella asked my brother.

Marcos' face lit up. 'Yes, I loved it. The bit when they go out together, and he's in love with her and tells her, "We're all made of paper".'

'Yes, that bit's really good … What did you think of the clues?'

'I really liked them … Do you think we really are made from paper?'

Estrella face showed her surprise. 'I don't know, maybe … cut to fit. What do you think you're made of?' she asked Marcos, while I sat there, completely excluded from their conversation.

'Well, I'm not plastic … I dunno … I live on the hillside … and Má's in jail. I think I'm made of wood. But before that I was paper.'

Estrella smiled. 'Let's be wood then: strong and shady, with our roots buried deep in the ground.'

They smiled at each other with such mutual understanding — I'd never seen my brother like that with anyone — all thanks to that book. At the end, Estrella turned to me, her cheeks pink.

'I've never had anyone to talk to about books. My friends don't really like reading.'

We sat chatting in the café for an hour. Towards the end, Estrella asked us if we thought we'd find our brother.

I didn't know how to respond, but in the end, I admitted to myself the truth I'd been unwilling to face since the day he disappeared.

'I don't think so, no. We probably won't find my brother.'

Marcos turned to me.

'Doesn't anyone know where he is?'

'Yeah, there are people who know where he is, but they'll never tell us.'

'How horrible,' said Estrella. 'But you can go and look for him, can't you? There are missing persons associations, for people who—'

'We're cannon fodder, Estrella. Who's going to look for *us*? They look for people who count, people who are at least a tiny little bit important. That's not us.'

'Not always.' And she looked at Marcos again, who was browsing some magazines.

One night on the way back home, we passed through El Rancho and found a red pick-up with chrome rims. Some boys about my age were sitting on the top smoking and drinking: the Zozaya cartel. One of them asked who we were, and I told him we lived up at the top.

'We're gonna be taking care of things round here,' he told me.

Then he put his hand on his waist where I could clearly see the handle of a pistol.

Perhaps it was because it was dark, but I could have sworn it was Fredy's.

Nothing ever appeared in the papers or on TV about Jeno or my brother's disappearance.

So when the lawyer informed us that the judge had made her decision, it was a bittersweet moment. We were happy to get Má back, but sad, because it still boiled down to the same old thing.

'It's all so ugly out here, but let's go get her,' I said to Marcos.

When we saw her emerge from the prison doors, I finally felt the weight of the hillside lift from my shoulders. Má hugged us, as if she'd been to another life and come back unchanged. She cried when she saw us, and I know she looked for Fredy among us out of habit.

We didn't go straight home. Má said she wanted to walk so we went into town. We sat in a small plaza off to one side of the Government Palace. She was silent for a while, weeping too.

When we got home, she said she was going to sleep, and boy, did she sleep. She woke up almost eighteen hours later. She was subdued for the rest of that day, but then she started to put the house back the way she liked it. None of the neighbours came out to meet her or welcome her back. We didn't go to school so we could stay with her.

Then, two weeks later, she told me what I had been expecting: I wouldn't be able to go on to study at the prepa because she needed me to work. We were standing on one of the slopes on the hillside looking out over the colonia and beyond that, the rest of the city, the chimneys of the foundry down at Fundidora Park, the city centre buildings, the enormous construction belonging to Cementos Mexicanos, the bend in the river.

'I'm sorry, mijo, but we ought to save so Marcos can keep studying, see how far he can go, as far as he possibly can.'

'And Fredy, Má?'

'We'll find him, son, I promise.'

'I have something for you,' I told her. That morning I'd been to unearth the hidden can from the warehouse. In keeping with my promise, I still hadn't opened it.

Má took it carefully. 'What's inside?'

'I dunno, but it's for you. I thought it'd be nice for you to open it when you got back. It's a surprise. I once found a canned hamburger.'

'A hamburger?!' I noticed she smiled for the first time since coming home. Then she fell silent, before she sighed and said, 'Let's open it when your brother comes home.'

It didn't take long for me to find work. I returned to the warehouse and Evaristo rehired me straightaway. People asked me about Miguel, but we never heard from him again. Má never had another boyfriend, or at least, she never brought anyone back home. It was all relatively OK. I finished high school and I've been working at the warehouse for nearly two years now. Má's still cleaning houses. Irma never returned to the colonia, but one weekend I went to look for her. She seemed really surprised to see me. Maybe something will happen there.

Sometimes I see Marcos studying and doing his homework up on the roof like I used to do. He always has his copy of *Ciudades de papel* close by; it's his most prized possession. He's read it about six times. Sometimes I give him some money to buy more books. We discovered a man down at the flea market who sells old novels for twenty or thirty pesos. I think Marcos is treading a different path to us. *I'm made of wood*, he told us. I prefer to think that deep down, we're all men and women with roots. We cling tightly to the hillside, always just beneath a layer of earth. Some of our shoots emerge and become flowers, while some are covered with thorns.

What we have added to our lives is that whenever we have some money saved up, we go for a coffee in one of those posh places with air conditioning. We take Má with us and because of her dealings with her employers, she's usually the most relaxed one there. She sits herself in the most comfortable chair and orders a hot or a cold chocolate. If it's the weekend, she dozes off and starts snoring, and we have to wake her up.

Sometimes, later in the afternoons, we dance along to the rebajadas. And Fredy appears, he's there, dancing with us, although he quickly returns to the world up there. We keep searching for him, especially on Sundays when we roam the slopes, the caves, the places where the earth sinks and the wind tickles the ground. Raúl put us in touch with an association. It's been tough. I … Well, perhaps it's best to stop here.

Some afternoons when I'm waiting at the bus stop on the Eloy Cavazos Avenue, I look at the road, where it begins. Only the road. Following it all the way up. A line lost among the hillside, paved in some places, but not in others. The road that climbs, starting off nearly twenty metres wide before narrowing, to nine, to eight to six. As it emerges onto the plateau, past the clogged-up drains and the piles of waste that keep growing as there's no truck to clear it away. The road where the women sell what they can, where the dogs mate at will and where the kids play football. The road begins to turn to earth because the budget didn't stretch any further. The road becomes footpaths, so many footpaths, where there's rubbish, homes thrown down by the hand of God, roof after roof of corrugated metal, tyres, more waste, until the path reaches the very last house in the neighbourhood. Ours.

Where we keep searching for him.

Monterrey, 30 August 2020
International Day of the Victims of Enforced Disappearance